Modern Indian Short Stories

THREE CROWNS BOOKS

Poetry
Keki N. Daruwalla: *Crossing of Rivers*
Nissim Ezekiel: *Hymns in Darkness*
Shiv K. Kumar: *Subterfuges*
R. Parthasarathy: *Rough Passage*
R. Parthasarathy (ed.): *Ten Twentieth-Century Indian Poets*
A. K. Ramanujan: *Selected Poems*

Drama
J. P. Clark: *Ozidi*
J. P. Clark: *Three Plays*
R. Sarif Easmon: *Dear Parent and Ogre*
Athol Fugard: *Boesman and Lena*
J. C. de Graft: *Sons and Daughters*
J. C. de Graft: *Through a Film Darkly*
Girish Karnad: *Hayavadana*
Howard McNaughton (ed.): *Contemporary New Zealand Plays*
Sonny Oti: *The Old Masters*
Ola Rotimi: *The Gods are not to Blame*
Ola Rotimi: *Kurunmi*
Ola Rotimi: *Our Husband's Gone Mad Again*
Ola Rotimi: *Ovonramwen Nogbaisi*
Badal Sircar: *Evam Indrajit*
Wole Soyinka: *A Dance of the Forests*
Wole Soyinka: *Kongi's Harvest*
Wole Soyinka: *The Lion and the Jewel*
Wole Soyinka: *The Road*
Joris Wartemburg: *The Corpse's Comedy*

Fiction
U. R. Anantha Murthy: *Samskara*
Obi B. Egbuna: *Daughters of the Sun and Other Stories*
David Umobuarie: *Black Justice*

Non-fiction
Arnold Apple: *Son of Guyana*

MODERN INDIAN SHORT STORIES

Edited with an introduction
by

SAROS COWASJEE

Professor of English, University of Regina

and

SHIV K. KUMAR

Distinguished Visiting Professor of English,
University of Oklahoma

CALCUTTA
OXFORD UNIVERSITY PRESS
DELHI   BOMBAY   MADRAS

Oxford University Press, Walton Street, Oxford OX2 6DP

NEW YORK TORONTO
DELHI BOMBAY CALCUTTA MADRAS KARACHI
PETALING JAYA SINGAPORE HONG KONG TOKYO
NAIROBI DAR ES SALAAM
MELBOURNE AUCKLAND

and associates in
BERLIN IBADAN

First published 1983
Second impression 1988

Printed in India by offset
by S. K. Seal at Pressagents Private Ltd. 2 Bidhan Sarani,
Calcutta 6 and published by S.K. Mookerjee, Oxford University Press,
Faraday House, Calcutta 13

Contents

Introduction

The genesis of the Indian short story can be traced to the *Puranas*, the *Panchatantra* and the *Jataka* tales. Ingeniously conceived and skilfully structured, most of these stories, both about human beings and animals, offer an inexhaustible source of pleasure even to the contemporary reader. But the modern Indian short story in English is about forty years old and it came to India from the West. It came at a time when it had already broken from the narrow confines of its origin and extended itself to encompass life in all its complexity.

Even as early as the turn of the century, writers found defining the short story a difficult task. Brander Matthews in 'The Philosophy of the Short-Story' is at pains to show the many aspects in which the short story differs from the novel: unity of impression, conciseness, sense of form, etc. But the differences between the novel and the short story in our own time are no longer as distinct and pronounced as they used to be. Generally speaking, a short story differs from the novel in its 'singleness of effect' and in its brevity. But here, too, there are exceptions. Joseph Conrad's highly acclaimed *Heart of Darkness* is occasionally studied as a short story. But it is longer by a few thousand words than Albert Camus' novel *The Outsider* and does not have the 'singleness of effect' of the latter.

The problem is not of defining the short story or agreeing on what it should or should not be. The essential problem is of arriving at a criterion by which this sophisticated form can be evaluated and enjoyed. Eudora Welty's expectation of a good short story is significant. Circumventing the question of style, mood, atmosphere, originality, ingenuity and the like (all of which are no doubt important and add to the final effect), she goes straight to what is the most important feature of the short story. Writing in *The Atlantic Monthly* of February–March 1949, she observed, 'So the first thing we see about a story is its mystery. And in the best stories, we return at the last to see

mystery again. Every good story has mystery—not the puzzle kind, but the mystery of allurement. As we understand the story better, it is likely that the mystery does not necessarily decrease; rather it simply grows more beautiful.'

Every story in this anthology fulfils this criterion, be it an overtly straightforward narrative as Ruskin Bond's 'The Night Train at Deoli' or Bhabani Bhattacharya's more complex attempt to fathom the human psyche, 'The Faltering Pendulum'. Bond's story has the distinction of being the only love story in the volume. At a cursory glance, it is about a shy, sentimental boy's longing for a girl he hardly knows. But a close reading of the story will reveal that it deals with the perennial human conflict between dream and reality. 'The Faltering Pendulum' is, on the surface, a tale of human loneliness, but it goes beyond it to explore the unconscious human mind. Much in the same way Khwaja Ahmad Abbas' 'Sparrows' is not about birds but about the human need for love; and R. K. Narayan's 'Dasi the Bridegroom' suggests the wide gulf that always separates illusion from reality. The human predicament, the meaning concealed behind the obvious, is the hallmark of each story and a pertinent reason for its inclusion.

Though no two stories in this anthology are singularly alike in theme, they show a marked preference for problems confronting present-day India. At least half of the stories included here deal with poverty. Mulk Raj Anand's 'Old Bapu' is a study in destitution; the stories of Narayan, Bhattacharya and Abbas portray characters who find it difficult to make both ends meet. Anita Desai's 'A Devoted Son' touches, among other things, on the intricate father–son relationship in India; Khushwant Singh's 'Karma' and Anand's 'Duty' both show the debasement of Indian character under British rule. Even Bond's 'The Night Train at Deoli' obliquely touches on the problems of the boy–girl relationship in a society which frowns upon even innocent pre-marital friendship. Manohar Malgonkar's 'Bachcha Lieutenant' is about the only story where the social context is not significantly Indian and where no change is sought in the Indian attitude to life.

Irony permeates Indian fiction as does no other single factor. Singh and Anand, both realists, have no patience with the contradictions and superstitions that pervade much of Indian life. Their attack is frontal and forthright, both making extensive use of satire to achieve their ends. Singh's 'The Mark of Vishnu' is an unconcealed attack on superstition and the blind reverence of the orthodox Hindu, while Anand's 'Duty' and 'Old Bapu' are a blatant exposure of the pettiness of a people that makes an exorbitant claim on its humanity. Narayan, too, makes use of irony, but he has come to terms with the foibles of human existence and censures them with good-humoured cynicism. Irony and satire are the most difficult to wield, and the Indian writers' success with them is a measure of their accomplishment.

It is in the matter of language—of adapting the English language as a medium of expression to convey Indian thought and sensibility—that Indian fiction has acquired a characteristic flavour of its own. The adaptation has taken two forms: first, the interpolation of well-known Indian words into English to convey an atmosphere of Indianness; second, and more daring, the translation of idioms and phrases from the Indian languages into English, even at the risk of violating English syntax and usage. Though some credit for the distinctive use of Indian words, phrases and idioms must go to Sochee Chunder Dutt and Lal Behari Day, it was only with the novels of Anand and Raja Rao in the thirties that Indian English came into its own. Anand was the first Indian writer of English to see the inadequacy of Standard English to cope with the Indian psyche, and Rao was the first to state this. 'The telling has not been easy', he wrote in his Preface to *Kanthapura* (1938). 'One has to convey in a language that is not one's own the spirit that is one's own. One has to convey the various shades and omissions of a certain thought-movement that looks maltreated in an alien language. I use the word "alien", yet English is not really ar alien language to us. It is the language of our intellectual make-up . . . but not of our emotional make-up. We are all instinctively bilingual, many of us writing in our language and in English. We cannot write like the English. We should not.'

Not all will agree with Raja Rao. Narayan has found the Queen's English adequate to reveal Indian life in all its diversity, and his use of Standard English is a rebuff to those insistent on forging a new medium of expression. 'It [English] has served my purpose admirably, of conveying unambiguously the thoughts and acts of a set of personalities, who flourish in a small town located in a corner of South India.' There are also others, like Anita Desai and Bond, who have refused to take liberties with the language. But the success that Anand and Rao have had, despite criticism from purists, has more or less ensured that Indian English has found its roots as firmly as have Irish or American English.

Acknowledgements

Acknowledgements are due to the following for permission to include stories in this anthology:

To the author for 'Duty' from *The Barbers' Trade Union and Other Stories*, and 'Old Bapu' from *The Power of Darkness and Other Stories* by Mulk Raj Anand; to Hind Pocket Books and the author for 'The Faltering Per.dulum' from *Steel Hawk and Other Stories* by Bhabani Bhattacharya; to Indian Thought Publications and the author for 'The Martyr's Corner' from *Lawley Road and Other Stories*, and 'Dasi the Bridegroom' from *An Astrologer's Day and Other Stories* by R. K. Narayan; to Oxford University Press and the author for 'The True Story of Kanakapala, Protector of Gold' and 'Javni' from *The Cow of the Barricades and Other Stories* by Raja Rao; to Orient Paperbacks and the author for 'Bachcha Lieutenant' from *Bombay Beware* by Manohar Malgonkar; to the author for 'Sparrows', originally published in *Indian Literature* (London), by Khwaja Ahmad Abbas; to the author for 'Karma' and 'The Mark of Vishnu' from *The Mark of Vishnu and Other Stories* by Khushwant Singh; to the author for 'The Night Train at Deoli' by Ruskin Bond; to William Heinemann Ltd and the author for 'A Devoted Son' from *Games at Twilight and Other Stories* by Anita Desai.

MULK RAJ ANAND

Mulk Raj Anand was born in Peshawar in 1905 and was educated at the universities of Punjab and London. After earning his Ph.D. in philosophy in 1929, Anand began writing notes for T. S. Eliot's *Criterion*. Success came to him with the publication of his first novel, *Untouchable*, in 1935. Since then he has written some twenty works of fiction, including seven volumes of short stories. Best known for *Coolie* (1936) and the trilogy *The Village* (1939), *Across the Black Waters* (1940) and *The Sword and the Sickle* (1942), his most impressive work, nevertheless, is *Private Life of an Indian Prince* (1953). Since 1946, Anand has made Bombay his home. He edits the art magazine, *Marg*, and takes a vital interest in the country's literary and cultural life. Writing is still his main preoccupation, and he is currently working on a monumental autobiographical novel, entitled *The Seven Ages of Man*. Of these, three volumes have so far been published.

'Duty', first published by John Lehmann in *New Writing* in 1938, best illustrates Anand's view of how people in India 'extract pain from one another'. Mangal Singh, a constable on point-duty on a scorching summer day, takes shelter under a kikar tree as he waits for another constable to come and relieve him. He falls into a half-sleep when a sub-inspector stops by and canes him for dozing while on duty. Smarting under the pain of the beating, Mangal Singh vents his anger on a herdsman (whom he beats mercilessly) for failing to keep his donkeys from entering the Mall Road. The story not only reveals the brutality of the police, but it also successfully evokes an atmosphere of heat and dust.

'Old Bapu', a much later story, has none of the violence of the former in theme and treatment. Old Bapu, an untouchable who looks much older than he really is, treads seven miles in the sweltering heat to seek road-repair work. On reaching his destination he finds that the contractor is unwilling to hire him and sends him away. Old Bapu next stops at a pan-biri shop where, after quenching his thirst for water, he begins to examine his shrivelled face in a mirror. From here as well he is asked to move on: ' "Oh ja, ja, ahead," said the pan-biri wallah. "Don't

break my glass by showing it your ugly old face!" ' Anand
seems to say that the callousness of people towards others is as
threatening as their deliberate cruelty.

Duty

The midday sun blasts everything in the Indian summer: it
scorches the earth till its upper layers crack into a million
fissures; it sets fire to the water till the lakes and pools and
swamps bubble, evaporate and dry up; it shrivels up the lives
of birds, beasts and flowers; it burns into one like red pepper
and leaves one gasping for breath with a bulging tongue till one
spends one's time looking for some shady spot for even the most
precarious shelter.

Mangal Singh, the policeman who had been posted on duty
at the point where the branch road from the village of Vadala
enters the Mall Road of Chetpur, had taken shelter under the
sparse foliage of a kikar tree beyond the layers of white dust,
after having stood in the sun for five and a half hours since dawn.
In a little while sepoy Rahmat-Ullah would come and relieve
him, and he felt that he could cool down a little and prepare to
go to the barracks.

The sun was penetrating even the leaves of the wayside trees,
and there was not much comfort in the humid airless atmosphere, but after the crackling heat of the open, Mangal felt that
this comparative shade was a blessing.

He was not, of course, like the delicate Lallas, rich Hindu
merchants, who rode out into the gardens early in the morning
and withdrew after 'eating' the fresh air at sunrise and never
appeared till sunset, sitting in the laps of their wives drinking
milk-water or lying sprawled about on the front boards of their
shops under the cool air of electric fans. . . . No, he didn't say
as they would: 'I go for a pice worth of salt, bring me a palan-
quin.' Nor could he 'quench his thirst by drinking dew'. No,
he was proud that he came from strong peasant stock and

was a hardy policeman who could rough it: indeed, this police
service was not active enough for him and he felt it a pity that
he had not become a real sepoy; for there was more pay in the
paltans and there were better uniforms, also free mufti and free
rations. So he had heard after he had put the mark of his thumb
down and joined the police force—but once done cannot be
undone. And it was the blessing of the Gurus, as there was little
chance of earning any extra money in the military; while,
apart from the fifteen rupees' pay, there were other small sums
so long as confectioners continued to mix milk with water and
so long as there was a murder or two in the prostitutes' bazaar,
and so long as there were respectable Lallas who would pay
rather than have their names mentioned. . . . Why, even here
on point-duty in the waste land—'your own is your own and
another's is also yours'. For if the peasants offered tokens of
grain and butter and sugar to the Munshi at the customs house,
then why not to the police? That skinny little Babu at the
octroi post had not the strong arm of the sepoy to protect them
when they were being looted by the thugs in the market. . . . He
knew. After wisdom the club. If only he had been able to pay
a nazar to the Tehsildar he would never have lost his land to
Seth Jhinda Ram. . . . But God's work was well done, man's
badly. And, truly, if he had not pressed the limbs of the land-
lord he would never have got the recommendation to join the
police. And you learnt a great deal in the service of the Sarkar.
And there was nothing better than service: no worry, and there
was so much izzat in it that these very cowardly city folk who
laughed at you if you were a peasant joined their hands in
obeisance to you if you wielded a truncheon. And the rustics
who had no notion of discipline or duty could be made to obey
authority with the might of the stave, and if they didn't obey
that, the fear of the handcuff—even a daring robber like Barkat
Ali could not escape because one could blow the whistle and call
the entire police force out. And the Sarkar is truly powerful.
Like Alamgir, it leaves no fire in the hearth, nor water in the
jar, to bring a man to justice. . . .

He glanced at his dust-covered feet in the regulation shoes of rough cow-hide, even as he congratulated himself on his lucky position as a member of the much-feared police service and wished he had really been in the army, for there the sepoys had boots given them. His puttees too were old and faded and there was something loose about the khaki uniform with the black belt. The uniform of the army was so tight-fitting. Perhaps the whistle-chain and the truncheon improved this and the red-and-blue turban was nice, but—he lifted his hand to caress the folds of his head-dress and to adjust it, as it was heavy and got soaked with the sweat that flowed from his fuming scalp burdened by long hair on the lower edges. . . .

The sun poured down a flood of fire on the earth, and it seemed as if the desolate fields covered with dense brown thickets and stalks of grass and cacti were crackling like cinders and would soon be reduced to ashes. A partridge hummed in its nest somewhere and a dove cooed from the tree overhead, giving that depth to the shade which fills the air with long, endless silences and with the desolate peace of loneliness.

Mangal Singh drifted a few steps from where he was standing and halted on a spot where the shade was thicker than it was anywhere else under the kikar trees. And, blowing a hot breath, he cupped his palms over the knob of his stave and leaned his chin on the knuckles of his joined hands and stood contemplating the scene with half-closed eyes like a dog who rests his muzzle on his front paws and lies in wait for his prey.

Layers of white-sheeted mist floated past his eyes in the sun-soaked fields, the anguish of a thousand heat-singed bushes, while the parched leaves of the hanging boughs of the wayside trees rustled at the touch of a scorching breeze.

One breath, a thousand hopes, they say, and there never comes a day without evening—but it would be very difficult to walk down to the barracks through this terrible heat. And he wished his duty was not up, that someone could fetch his food for him and that he could borrow a charpai from the octroi and go to sleep in the grove of neem trees by the garden of Rais Jagjiwan Das, or sit and talk to the grass-cutter's wife who had breasts like turnips. Only Rahmat-Ullah had an eye on her too, and he was sure to be here, as he preferred the desolate afternoon, thinking that he might get a chance when no one was about.

'I will have to walk back to the lines,' he muttered to himself and yawned. He felt heavy and tired at the prospect and his legs seemed to weaken from the knowledge of the unending trudge of three miles. He shook his head and tried to be alert, but the invisible presence of some overwhelming force seemed to be descending on him and his heavy-lidded eyes were closing against his will. He took a deep breath and made another effort to open his eyes wide through the drowsy stupor of the shade that weighed down from the trees. For a moment his body steadied and his eyes half opened. But how hateful was the glare, and how cruel, how meaningless, was life outside. . . . And what peace, what quiet below the trees, beneath the eyes. . . .

If a God should be standing here he could not help closing his eyes for a minute, he felt; and sleep came creeping into his bones with a whiff of breeze that was like a soft beauty retreating coyly before the thousand glares of the torrid sun which burnt so passionately above the silent fields. . . . The heat seemed to be melting the fat in his head and to be blinding his eyes, and he let himself be seduced by the placid stillness into a trance of half-sleep. . . .

Through sleepy eyes he was conscious of the whispering elements as he dozed, and his body still stood more or less erect, though his head was bent on the knuckles of his hand above the stave, and the corners of his mouth dribbled slightly. . . .

'Shoop . . . shoop . . . shoop . . .' a snake seemed to lash his face at the same time as he saw the soothing vision of a dim city through the stealthy corners of whose lanes he was passing suavely into a house was effaced. . . .

'Shoop . . . shoop. . . .'

He came to suddenly and saw Thanedar Abdul Kerim standing before him, his young face red with anger under the affected Afghan turban, his tall lanky form tight-stretched, a cane in his hand, and his bicycle leaning against his legs. . . .

'Wake up! Wake up, you ox of a Sikh! Is it because it is past twelve that your senses have left you?'

Mangal reeled, then steadied himself, his hands climbing automatically to his turban which had been shaken by the Inspector's onslaught.

'Shoop . . . shoop,' the cane struck his side again and stung his skin like a hundred scorpions. And a welter of abuse fell upon his ears: 'Bahin chod, the D.S.P. might have passed, and you are supposed to be on *duty*. Wake up and come to your senses, Madar chod!'

Quite involuntarily Mangal's right hand left the turban and shot up to his forehead in a salute, and his thick, trembling lips phewed some hot stale breath: 'Huzoor Mai-bap.'

'You eat the bread of illegality,' the Thanedar shouted. 'I will be reprimanded and my promotion stopped, you swine!'

And he lifted his cane to strike Mangal again, but the sepoy was shaking with fright so that his stave dropped from his hand.

Mangal bent and picked up his lathi.

'Go and be on your point-duty!' ordered the Thanedar sternly and, putting his foot on the pedal, rode shakily away on his bicycle.

Mangal walked out of the shade, his shins and thighs still trembling and his heart thumping in spite of himself, though he was less afraid than conscience-stricken for neglecting his duty.

The heat of the sun made the skin of his face smart with a sharp pain where the perspiration flowed profusely down his neck. He rubbed his hand across it and felt the sweat tingle like a raw wound.

He shook himself and his head twitched, and he looked about in order to see if anyone had seen him being beaten. He wanted to bear the pain like a man. But his eyes, startled by the suddenness with which they had opened, were full of a boiling liquid that melted into fumes as he raised his head.

His throat was parched dry and he coughed with an effort so that his big brown face above the shaggy beard reddened. Then he paused to spit on the road and felt his legs trembling and shaking more than ever. He twisted his face in the endeavour to control his limbs and lunged forward. . . .

'Ohe, may you die, ohe asses, ohe, may you die,' came a voice from behind him.

As he turned round he saw a herd of donkeys come stampeding up the road in a wild rush, which became wilder as their driver trotted fast behind them in an attempt to keep them from entering the Mall Road at that pace.

For a moment the cloud of dust the herd had raised on the sides of the deeply rutted Vadala Road obscured Mangal's view of the man, but then suddenly he could hear him shouting: 'Ohe, may you die, asses!'

Mangal ran with his stave upraised in a wild scurry towards the driver of the stampeding donkeys, scattering them helter-skelter till some of them cantered the more quickly into the Mall and the others turned back and came to a standstill. He caught the driver up before the man had escaped into a ditch by the banana field. And, grinding a half-expressed curse between his teeth, he struck him with his stave hard, hard, harder, so that the blows fell edgewise on a donkey's neck, on the driver's arms, on a donkey's back, on a donkey's head, on the man's legs. . . .

'Oh, forgive, Sarkar, it is not my fault,' the man shouted in an angry, indignant voice while he rubbed his limbs and spread his hands to ward off more blows.

'You, son of a dog,' hissed Mangal as he struck again and again, harder and harder as if he had gone mad, till his stave seemed to ring as a bamboo stick does when it is splitting into shreds.

From *The Barbers' Trade Union
and Other Stories*, 1944

Old Bapu

They say, in our parts, that, at the solemn moment of death, even when death is sudden, every man sees the whole of his past underneath his skull.

Old Bapu fancied, as he walked along towards the Gurgaon bazaar, that his end had come. And, as though by the power of this suggestion, the various worlds rose behind his head, way back in the distance of time, rather like balls of heat wrapped in mist, projections of the omnipotent sun that shone overhead, veiled and blurred by the haze of memory.

The city was still a mile away, and the flesh of his feet burnt where it touched the new, hot metalled road through the holes in the shoes. And the sweat poured down across the furrows on his face, especially through the two sharp channels which stretched from the nose towards the chin, like rivulets flooding a fallow field. . . . A bluish shimmer flickered across his vision of the houses ahead.

As though compelled by the discomfort of slogging on foot and the weakness in his joints after the seven miles' tread from Shikohpur, he felt his body evaporating, and his soul in the state of that lightness which disclosed the saga of his past life, going round and round in his cranium. And as he felt near enough to exhaustion and death, and yet did not want to die ('May Ishwar banish such a thought from my head,' he prayed), the agitation of his nerves produced the aberration of a phantasma, like the red stars over a toothache. . . .

'I am not old,' he said to himself in the silent colloquy of his soul with his body. 'The boys call me "old Bapu" because I am older than them. . . . The caste Hindu urchins have no respect for the untouchable elders anyhow. And their fathers want to throw everyone of us into the garbage pit to use as manure for better harvests. . . . But I do not want to die. . . . Hey Ishwar!'

The saga of his life forced itself into his head, in spite of his protests, in several minute details, bits of memories entangled with the awkward drone of heat overhead, drumming into his ears.

He was a child, sitting by the revolving spinning wheel of his mother, disturbing the iron needle, because she would not get up and give him the stale bread and pickle. . . . Little specks of wool arose from the cotton in her hand, soft as the sighs which she uttered in despair at his mischief—or was it because there was no roti in the basket inside? . . . And then she awoke from the trance of her eyes, rivetted on the thread of the takla and said: 'Acha, wait, tiny, I will go and borrow some food for you from the mother of Ram Dutt. . . .' And while she was gone, and he played about with the spinning wheel, against her strict injunctions, a rat gnawing in his belly. . . .

Lighter than air, his body proceeded on the way to Gurgaon bazaar, flitting into a cloud of unknowing. He walked almost with his eyes closed, seeing himself as a small boy singing a song, against the counterpoint of the wheel of the well, as he drove the bullocks round and round. . . . And the big boys came and pulled his slight frame from the seat and began to take a ride on the shaft. And, as he sought, with his tiny hands, to grip them, they thrust him away and threw him into the well, where he shrieked in panic, holding on to the chain of earthen vessels, while they all ran away, and he slowly climbed up, exhausted and dying. . . .

Drifting from that early-death into life, he felt he could ward off the present feeling of weakness in his limbs, and, perhaps, he would be lucky, with at least half a day's work.

'Stay with me son, when you go from me I shall die!' he heard his mother's words beckon from the mythical memories of his adolescence. 'Your father went soon after you were born, and you will have no one after I am gone. . . .' And he recalled that in his eagerness to work in the fields, and to become a tall man and not remain the small creature he was, he had gone away that afternoon, and then he had come home to find his mother dead. . . . His spirit tried to fly away from the ugly thought of his betrayal of her, but its wings were rooted in his coarse little body, and in spite of a violent cough, which he excited in his

throat, even as he spat on the dust a globule of phlegm, the soul
held the vision of his mother's dead face, eyes dilated and the
teeth showing in the terrordark of their hut. . . .

'May Ishwar keep her soul in heaven!' he prayed. And, as
though by magic, his treason was forgotten in the next few
footsteps. . . .

But even as he mopped the sweat off his face with the forepaws
of his right hand, the scales seemed to lift from his eyes, and his
soul was face to face with the forepaws of his right hand, and
then with a monster, his Uncle Dandu Ram, who shouted: 'I
am tired of you! Good for nothing scoundrel! Everyone is tired
of you! Inauspicious bastard! You cannot plough the fields well!
Nor can you look after the cattle! Go and eat dung elsewhere—
there is no food for you in my house.'

The bushes on the roadside exuded the same smell in the
parched heat, which had come from the clumps of grass amid
the mounds and hollows of Shikohpur where he had wandered,
half crazy with hunger and the beatings which the boys gave
him, like birds of prey falling upon a weaker member of the
flock. . . . O the cruelty of it! And the laceration of abuse and
bitter words! . . . And Dandu had taken his half bigha of land
saying, 'You are an idiot, incapable of looking after it!'

The lavamist of heat pressed down over his eyes and half shut
them through the glare. The mood of his soul became more and
more seraphic, accepting the vision of the crusts of black bread
and lentils which he loved so much, after the work when he was
engaged as a field labourer by some prosperous Hindu farmer
of the upper caste.

Only the anxiety of not getting work today began to gnaw into
his being as the houses of Gurgaon loomed up fifty hands away.

A man mounted on a bicycle brushed past him from ahead
after tinkling his bell furiously. And Bapu realized that he must
be careful in town if he wanted to escape death.

The city was a labyrinth of jagged shops, tall houses and
rutted roads. And waves of men coursed along the edges of the
streets, receding, returning towards the hawkers, who sat with
condiments and fruits and vegetables before them.

The broken asphalt attracted him. He had worked on road-making. Fetching stones and breaking them. So much cement was put down on certain roads that they never broke. But here, the contractors were paid, to make pavements hard, and to fill the ruts every season, for after every rainy season the ruts reappeared.

That was the work he had come to ask for.

Suddenly, he turned in the direction of Model Town where the Sikh contractor, Ram Singh, lived.

In his heart there was an old cry of fear at the potential temper of this man, which had always cowed him down. His glance fell at his fingertips which had been blunted through hammering stones. The congealed flesh of corns at the ends of the fingers gave the effect of toughness and he felt strong to see them, knowing that he was capable of the hardest work. . . . Distant, more distant seemed to grow the contractor's house with the courtyard, even though he had entered Model Town.

Sardar Ram Singh was sitting on a charpai under the neem tree, the bun of his hair a little loose from sleep.

Bapu joined his hands and stood looking at the god.

'Aoji Bapu!' the contractor said surlily breaking the edge of his taciturnity.

The vibration of each part of Ram Singh's face made Bapu's soul shudder, and he could not speak.

'Ohe speak—what do you want?' Ram Singh asked, fanning himself the while with a hand fan.

The voice surged up in Bapu even as he breathed deeply to sigh. But the sound would not come out.

Ram Singh stared at him for a prolonged moment.

Bapu made a sign with his hands and opened his mouth to say: 'Work.'

'Ohe ja ja, oldie! You can't work, with that frame of yours! . . . Doing half work for full pay! Besides the rains have not yet abated. Don't be deceived by this sunshine. . . . The big rains have yet to come! . . .'

A low and horrible sound was in Bapu's belly, and he felt that he was being strangled by the serpent of sweat that flowed down to his neck from the face. His lips twitched, and the tone of the contractor's words sounded like the news of doom in his ears.

'How old are you?' Ram Singh asked eyeing him with seemingly cynical indifference.

'The earthquake in Kangra—when it came, I was born!'

The contractor was startled. He smiled, and, surveying Bapu's frame, said: 'About fifty years ago—but you look seventy. Life in our country is ebbing away. The workmen seem to have no strength left. Look at you, two-legged donkey that you are! One of your legs seems to be shrivelled, while the other feeble one seems to be waiting to drag it on. . . . All of us have become lame and go hopping, tottering and falling, wishing for the Sarkar to carry us forward. Comic and undignified and shameless! . . .'

'No land, no harvests!' Bapu said desperately. 'And—' And he stretched out his hands.

'Acha, take this and go!' the contractor ground the words and looked away. 'Let me rest. Take this . . .' he took a nickel piece and threw it at Bapu.

The labourer bent his eyes over his hands, joined them in supplication and gratitude and still stood.

'Ja, don't stand on my head!' Ram Singh shouted. 'The work on the roads will begin when the rains are over!'

Bapu was more frightened of his agony of frustration than of the contractor's words. He controlled the tears in his eyes and slid away on ambling feet.

The prolonged burbling of a beetle from the slime in a drain stirred a feeling of terrible self-pity in him. He wanted to drink some water to avoid breaking down. And, seeing a lone pan-biri stall, tucked away between the walls of two different houses, a little further away, he headed towards it.

His eyes were almost closed. His lips twitched against his will. And he was like a somnambulist, walking blindly towards some unknown goal. The fact that he had a nickel piece in his hands warded off the feeling of death that had preoccupied him on the approach towards Gurgaon. Now, he only felt the precariousness of the dim future, in which his good or bad deeds would rotate in the inexorable rhythm of work and no work.

'Pani!' he said to the shopkeeper, joining his hands, first in greeting, then unfolding them as a cup.

The pan-biri wallah eyed him suspiciously, then relaxed in the face of the Sun's merciless stare, and began to pour water into the stranger's cupped hands from a brass jug.

Bapu drank and belched his fill. Then he caressed his face with his moist hands and touched his eyes with the water on his fingertips. The cool touch of liquid seemed to revive him.

And, as though from some instinct for seeking reassurance, he looked into the mottled mirror that hung down from the pan-biri shop. He had not looked at himself in such a glass for years. He saw that his face was shrivelled up, lined with the wrinkles which had been sharpened by hard work in his youth, and many small lines criss-crossed the corners of his eyes, his forehead, his jowl and neck. And a greyish pallor covered the visage, more than the abject anxiety to please the contractor, rather like the colour of death which he had apprehended as he had walked along the road. The shock of the old face disturbed him and he turned away from the mirror. 'About seventy years!' Ram Singh said. So he turned towards the mirror again.

'Oh ja, ja, ahead,' said the pan-biri wallah. 'Don't break my glass by showing it your ugly old face!'

Old Bapu ambled along ahead, hoping to buy four annas worth of corn to sustain himself in the illusion of youth.

From *The Power of Darkness
and Other Stories*, 1959

BHABANI BHATTACHARYA

Born in 1906 in Bhagalpur, Bihar, Bhabani Bhattacharya studied history at the University of Patna, and then at the University of London from where he graduated with a Ph.D. in 1934. During his student days in London he began contributing articles to British periodicals, and continued writing for magazines and papers on his return to India in 1935. In 1947 he published *So Many Hungers!*, and since then he has built for himself a strong reputation with novels such as *Music for Mohini* (1952), *He Who Rides a Tiger* (1954), *A Goddess Named Gold* (1960), *Shadow from Ladakh* (1966), for which he received the Sahitya Akademi Award, *Steel Hawk and Other Stories* (1968), and his most recent, *A Dream in Hawaii* (1978). In addition to these novels, Bhattacharya has translated the works of Tagore and written books on Gandhi and Indian history. He has travelled widely and has lectured at universities in the United States, Europe, Australia and New Zealand. He lives in St Louis County, Missouri, U.S.A.

'The Faltering Pendulum' was first published in *Life and Letters* in 1950, and later included in Bhabani Bhattacharya's *Steel Hawk and Other Stories* (1968). On the surface it is a study in human loneliness, but it goes beyond that to touch the dark areas of the sub-conscious mind and the ambiguities of birth and death. An old woman in her final years acquires a goat 'youngling' and pumpkin seeds in exchange for rags. The goat becomes her sole companion; the pumpkin vine her hope in the renewal of life. The vine flowers but bears no fruit, and she sees in the plant's life a reflection of her own barren womanhood. Then one day the goat nibbles the vine and the enraged woman throttles her pet. As she wails the loss of her goat, a neighbour tells her of two small pumpkins hanging in the patch the goat had cleared in the vine. The anguish on her face turns to joy.

The Faltering Pendulum

From neighbouring stalls in the Tuesday haat of the village she purchased by a barter of rags the two objects that were to make the *motif* of her life for months to come: three ripe pumpkin seeds embedded in the flesh of a sliced crescent piece, and a month-old goat youngling.

She, the rag-woman, shuffled along the village path at dusk-fall, the pumpkin slice clutched in one hand, the little white goat (black edges about the eyes, like marks of collyrium) in the crook of the other arm. The goat craned its neck, sniffing the eatable. A lolling tongue emerged. The woman slapped the narrow face with the bony back of her palm. 'Have you no shame? Have you no feeling? Are you nothing but a fool goat?' She held her thin arms apart.

Even in that early hour she could see the vines grow out of the three pumpkin seeds, lithe-bodied vines outspread on reed thatch, with profuse gold-yellow flowers, and some flowers were mere ornament but others had in them the mother-urge of creating, and these bore fruit, the enormous fruit of the pumpkin growing out of a slip of a tender bright bloom. In a deep way it would be akin to her own inmost throb of fulfilment. The rag-woman eyed her new pet and gave it a long hard stare and said, 'Are you nothing but a fool goat?'

Her white hair thinning at the top lay drawn at the back of her head, coiled up in a petty bun. Her short slight frame stooped a little with the burdens of age and a temper. While she had grown in years there had been no mellowing of the stuff of her life, lone, no kin to stay with her, no consolation save in rags. Those rags, collected from door to door, were more than her living. Each had a meaning and a story. A smell of life clung on to the cast-off clothes of man and woman. Each had its own individual smell of life. The rag-woman lived with the smells. They kindled a zest in her and fed her fancies. With the rags of people strewn about her on the mud floor of her shack, she

projected herself, she spread out, among the people. Her alone-
ness was gone. She felt strangely soothed.

If only she could be rid of the core of temper, the hard nut
inside her, that had made her scorned and laughed at. As she
shuffled back from the market that day and drew close to the
shadowed mango grove skirting the weavers' settlement, her
furtive glance cast around and she addressed the inward nut,
'Keep still. Do not toss about. Keep still.'

'Baa-aa!' the goat cried, as though echoing the invocation.

'Baa-aa? What do you know about it, fool goat?'

'Moo-oo!' A soft pitying murmur, tremulous.

The woman drew her grey brows together, watchful, the
wrinkled face intent. And the odd wish-thought hit her then:
'He knows. He understands. No fool goat, this.'

'How hold my temper against the young devils who will come
dashing in a moment to pester me? What bones can put up with
such harrowing?' she confided to her animal and her eyes had
a hunted look while she hurried her feet, hoping to pass by
unseen.

'Rag hag!' shot out the inevitable cry and the grinning face
of a youngster peered from the dark of a tree-trunk screen.

'Keep still,' she muttered, desperate, to the hard core of her
temper. 'Do not toss about.' Her heart was beating wildly.

'Rag hag's got a puppy!' from another tree-trunk. And many
voices all about lifted together: 'Rag hag's got a puppy!'

'A goat, no puppy,' said the woman, hoarse, with violent
calm.

'Little white puppy. Rag hag's got a white puppy.' A
youngster sped out of cover and darted, hurtling close by the
woman, with a big yell.

'A goat,' shrilled the woman, fiercely turning round, holding
the animal aloft for all to see. 'Have maggots eaten your eye-
balls?'

A second youngster dashed up with a yell. 'Ho! Rag hag's
puppy will not walk; it rides on her, the white puppy.' And he
too shot by, passing his friend who was now racing back like an
excited colt.

'Your tongue will rot. Vultures will peck at your bones.'

'Ho!' cried the boys with the thoughtless cruelty of youth. 'Rag hag—mad hag!' And their mouths were hard, eyes ashine with mirth.

The woman, now utterly lost to reason, an abandoned flotsam on the sweeping tide of her fury, picked up a brickbat and flung it at the boys. 'The womb that bore you will be deadwood.' She dashed up crazily, fuming, throwing brickbats, the eyes in their deep sockets bulging fearfully.

So it went on for a minute, and then with one big shout of laughter and a final 'Rag hag . . . mad hag!' the boys, having had their grand fun, melted away in the deep dusk of the orchard. The woman looked this way and that, hurtling her last brickbats. 'Take this. Take more. Your skull will crack. Your mouths will spit blood. Take one more.'

Spent, gasping, she resumed her walk and as the tossing nut of her temper lay still, she hung her head in utmost shame.

'You saw?' she murmured to her pet. 'That angry thing rolled again in my belly.'

'Mmm!' agreed the animal.

'You heard? My tongue cursed the children, this vile filthy tongue. May it be torn out from its root.'

'Moo-oo!' came the bleat of sympathy.

He understood her! He felt for her! No fool goat. The ragwoman clasped the animal to her breast as if to fill an emptiness within. Her bleary eyes were wet. She felt soothed.

That was how the rag-woman started her new kinship with the goat youngling. She pattered to the animal all day long and revealed her suppressed heart. No one had ever cared to listen to her talk because of the temper in her and the keen edge of her tongue. Only the goat listened and answered in pity and listened again.

The three pumpkin seeds sprouted and the vines spread out. One died but the others grew fast. The rag-woman collected the black pellets of her animal's dung and cast them in her patch of earth to mingle with the soil and add their rich nurture to the growing vines. She hoped that the vines, fed on that dung, would imbibe some essential of the goat's being and would listen to the flow of her talk, and even if they could not answer with baa and maa, they would surely make response by the wag of a tendril, the swing of a leaf.

She was strangely close to the life of the vines, that lone despised woman of a remote Bengal village. For her they had a being. She could feel the rhythm of their growth and the movement of sap from rootlets deep in earth to the thrusting profusion of wide fresh-skinned leaves. She divided herself between her animal and her vines. Both had her in equal measure.

Then, one day, the blow fell.

The vines were in their first bloom. The rag-woman watched, athrill. Out of the sun-washed gold-yellow blooms fruit would come. Seeds—flowers—fruit—seeds, the complete life cycle, immutable. The first flowers came and went, fruitless. That often happened in the early stage and was not to be worried about. But it continued well beyond the normal span of time. New plump blooms burst forth every day, their profuse gold glittering in the hard sun. The blooms died. Not one pumpkin showed itself anywhere on the vines. The woman scanned the winding, twisted lengths every day with a flutter in her heart, peering under the clumps of leaves. In vain.

Barren! The two vines were barren!

The rag-woman, struck by the thought, stared aghast at the bright-flowered ones. She trembled and sank down on her knees and she knocked her head on the earth and grieved.

They were dead things, those vines. They had tricked her.

Some dream in her was shattered. For, she herself was a barren one. Widowed in middle age, not once had her womb-flower borne fruit in all the years when she had a husband. She was all deadwood inside. And she had entered the being of the young-limbed pumpkin vines, seeking some fulfilment. The vines had tricked her. It seemed that whatever she touched must become barren.

The temper in her tossed and rattled angrier than ever before, and her tongue renewed its razor edge.

Then it so happened that some folly came upon the goat one day and it grew reckless and flouted the woman, its mistress. She saw it calmly lopping up the leaves of the vine. 'Keep off!' she cried, but the goat's answer was challenging and mockful. Later, the goat was nibbling the vine again. Once more the woman warned it and dragged it away. In a half-hour the persistent goat was again pillaging the vine. Now the woman's temper came, a swift fire-burst. 'Dare you?' She clutched the goat's throat with the claw-like fingers of both hands. She pressed hard, gritting her gappy teeth in resistless fury, and pressed harder. 'Dare you?' When her fingers loosened, the goat dropped limply on the mud floor. It was dead. The rag-woman had throttled her pet.

She shook the inert body. Alarmed, she called the animal by its name. She felt for its breath. Then she sat awhile in a daze. At last the tears began to pour down her sunken cheeks and she wailed out, 'My goat, my goat!' The cry drew alarmed neighbours. They tried to revive the goat, splashing water on its face. Then they tried to soothe the woman and offered to buy her, helpless one, a new pet from the haat. But the woman beat her breast, knocked her head on the floor and kept on wailing, 'My goat, my goat!'

The day passed. An hour before dusk a young girl came running to the grief-stricken woman as she lay in bed and called out excitedly, 'The vines! Two little pumpkins, like ducks' eggs.' All the village knew about the barren vines; this girl had seized the rare chance of the woman's preoccupation with her pain to explore on her own.

The rag-woman looked up in puzzlement and it was some time before the words found their mark. Then she jerked up to her feet. She did not wipe the wet on her cheeks. Weak-kneed, she tottered after the girl.

'Look—' the girl cried and in that instant the woman was transformed. She gripped the girl's up-lifted arm with a quick thrust of her hand. 'Take heed, girl,' she cried, her voice trembling. 'Take heed not to point your finger at the younglings of pumpkin. Else, they will shrivel and fall. Growing, unripe things—fruit, flower-bud—all shrivel and die if pointed at. Nature's way. Take heed!'

And the girl nodded and closed her fingers tight lest, unwary, they pointed.

The goat had cleared up thick patches of leaves, and on a stripped tendril a tiny pumpkin hung. Another, a yard away. Oh, how could she have missed them?

Even in her deep anguish the rag-woman's tear-stained face beamed. The goat was dead, a white heap still lying on the mud floor. But the pumpkin vines had sprung to fruitful life, after their long barren dead-aliveness. A balance was achieved. The faltering pendulum had regained its swing.

From *Steel Hawk and Other Stories*, 1968

R. K. NARAYAN

One of the best known Indian English writers, R. K. Narayan was born in 1907 in Madras and graduated from Maharaja's College in Mysore. His first novel, *Swami and Friends*, appeared in 1935, and was greeted with a chorus of praise. 'It was Mr Narayan with his *Swami and Friends*', wrote Graham Greene, 'who first brought India, in the sense of the Indian population and the Indian way of life, alive to me.' Among his other works are *The Bachelor of Arts* (1937), *The Dark Room* (1938), *An Astrologer's Day and Other Stories* (1947), *Mr Sampath* (1949), *The Financial Expert* (1952), *The Guide* (1958), *The Man-eater of Malgudi* (1961), *A Horse and Two Goats* (1970) and *My Days* (1974). The Michigan State College Press began in 1953 to publish Narayan's works and thus introduced him to American readers. In 1958 he was given the Sahitya Akademi Award for *The Guide*.

'The Martyr's Corner' is taken from R. K. Narayan's *Lawley Road and Other Stories* (1956). The story illustrates Narayan's two cardinal qualities as a writer—his humanity and his gentle irony. Rama, 'the prince' among wayside caterers, owns a portable stall which he sets up every day at a corner near a cinema house. He does a flourishing business selling bondas and dosais. One day there is a riot and a person is killed at the spot where he sets his stall. The spot is declared holy ground, and Rama is pushed out as a memorial is erected to the dead man. Rama, with a fortitude characteristic of Narayan's characters, becomes a waiter in a restaurant and finds comfort in recalling 'I was once a hotel-owner myself.'

'Dasi the Bridegroom' is taken from Narayan's *An Astrologer's Day and Other Stories* (1947). Narrated dramatically, in a lucid style, the story suggests the wide gulf that always separates illusion from reality. As Dasi's dream of marrying a beautiful film star is shattered, he finds himself locked in a mental hospital. But he still tenaciously clings to his fantasy. What makes the story successful is its skilful blending of humour and pathos, smiles and tears.

The Martyr's Corner

Just at that turning between Market Road and the lane leading to the chemist's shop he had his establishment. If anyone doesn't like the word 'establishment', he is welcome to say so, because it was actually something of a vision spun out of air. At eight you would not see him, and again at ten you would see nothing, but between eight and ten he arrived, sold his goods, and departed.

Those who saw him thus remarked: 'Lucky fellow! He has hardly an hour's work a day and he pockets ten rupees—what graduates are unable to earn! Three hundred rupees a month!' He felt irritated when he heard such glib remarks, and said, 'What these folk do not see is that I sit before the oven practically all day frying all this stuff. . . .'

He got up when the cock in the next house crowed; sometimes it had a habit of waking up at three in the morning and letting out a shriek. 'Why has the cock lost its normal sleep?' Rama wondered as he awoke, but it was a signal he could not miss. Whether it was three o'clock or four, it was all the same to him. He had to get up and start his day.

At about 8.15 in the evening he arrived with a load of stuff. He looked as if he had four arms, so many things he carried about him. His equipment was the big tray balanced on his head, with its assortment of edibles, a stool stuck in the crook of his arm, a lamp in another hand, a couple of portable legs for mounting his tray. He lit the lamp, a lantern which consumed six pies' worth of kerosene every day, and kept it near at hand, since he did not like to depend only upon electricity, having to guard a lot of loose cash and a variety of miscellaneous articles.

When he set up his tray with the little lamp illuminating his display, even a confirmed dyspeptic could not pass by without throwing a look at it. A heap of bondas, which seemed puffed and big, but melted in one's mouth, dosais, white, round and limp, looking like layers of muslin, chappatis so thin that you could lift fifty of them on a little finger, duck's eggs, hard-boiled, resembling a heap of ivory balls, and perpetually boiling coffee on a stove. He had a separate aluminium pot in which he kept chutney, which went gratis with almost every item.

He always arrived in time to catch the cinema crowd coming out after the evening show. A pretender to the throne, a young scraggy fellow sat on the spot until he arrived and did business, but our friend did not let that unduly bother him. In fact he felt generous enough to say, 'Let the poor rat do his business when I am not there.' This sentiment was amply respected and the pretender moved off a minute before the arrival of the prince among caterers.

His customers liked him. They said in admiration: 'Is there another place where you can get coffee for six pies and four chappatis for an anna?' They sat around his tray, taking what they wanted. A dozen hands hovered about it every minute, because his customers were entitled to pick up, examine and accept their stuff after proper scrutiny.

Though so many hands were probing the lot, he knew exactly who was taking what: he knew by an extraordinary sense which of the jutka-drivers was picking up chappatis at a given moment; he could even mention his licence number; he knew that the stained hand nervously coming up was that of the youngster who polished the shoes of passers-by; and he knew exactly at what hour he would see the wrestler's arm searching for the perfect duck's egg, which would be knocked against the tray-corner before consumption.

His custom was drawn from the population swarming the pavement: the boot-polish boys, for instance, who wandered to and fro with brush and polish in a bag, endlessly soliciting, 'Polish, sir, polish!' Rama had a soft corner in his heart for the waifs. When he saw some fat customer haggling over the payment to one of these youngsters he felt like shouting, 'Give the poor fellow a little more. Don't grudge it. If you pay an anna more he can have a dosai and a chappati. As it is, the poor fellow is on half-rations and remains half-starving all day.'

It rent his heart to see their hungry, hollow eyes; it pained him to note the rags they wore; and it made him very unhappy to see the tremendous eagerness with which they came to him, laying aside their brown bags. But what could he do? He could not run a charity show; that was impossible. He measured out their half-glass of coffee correct to the fraction of an inch, but they could cling to the glass as long as they liked.

The blind beggar, who whined for alms all day in front of the big hotel, brought him part of his collection at the end of the day and demanded refreshment . . . and the grass-selling women. He disliked serving women; their shrill, loud voices got on his nerves. These came to him after disposing of head-loads of grass satisfactorily. And that sly fellow with a limp who bought a packet of mixed fare every evening and carried it to a prostitute-like creature standing under a tree on the pavement opposite.

All the coppers that men and women of this part of the universe earned through their miscellaneous jobs ultimately came to him at the end of the day. He put all this money into a little cloth bag, dangling from his neck under his shirt, and carried it home, soon after the night show started in the theatre and when he had satisfied himself that all his patrons had carried something inside to munch.

He lived in the second lane behind the market. His wife opened the door, throwing into the night air the scent of burnt oil which perpetually hung about their home. She snatched from his hands all his encumbrances, put her hand under his shirt to pull out his cloth bag, and counted the cash immediately. They gloated over it. 'Five rupees invested in the morning has brought us another five . . .' They ruminated on the exquisite mystery of this multiplication. She put back into his cloth bag the capital for further investment on the morrow, and carefully separated the gains and took them away to a little wooden box that she had brought from her parents' house years before.

After dinner, he tucked a betel leaf and tobacco into his cheek and slept on the pyol of his house, and had dreams of traffic constables bullying him to move on and health inspectors saying that he was spreading all kinds of diseases and depopulating the city. But fortunately in actual life no one bothered him very seriously. He gave an occasional packet of his stuff to the traffic constable going off duty, or to the health department menial who might pass that way.

The health officer no doubt came and said, 'You must put all this under a glass lid, otherwise I shall destroy it all some day. . . . Take care!' But he was a kindly man who did not pursue any matter, but wondered in private, 'How his customers survive his food, I can't understand! I suppose people build up a sort of immunity to such poisons, with all that dust blowing on it, and the gutter behind. . . .' Rama no doubt violated all the well-accepted canons of cleanliness and sanitation, but still his customers not only survived his fare but seemed actually to flourish on it, having consumed it for years without showing signs of being any the worse for it.

Rama's life could probably be considered a most satisfactory one, without agitation or heart-burn of any kind. Why could it not go on for ever endlessly, till the universe itself cooled off and perished, when by any standard he could be proved to have led a life of pure effort? No one was hurt by his activity and money-making, and not many people could be said to have died of taking his stuff; there were no more casualties through his catering than, say, through the indifferent municipal administration.

But such security is unattainable in human life. The gods grow jealous of too much contentment anywhere and they show their displeasure all of a sudden. One night, when he arrived as usual at his spot, he found a babbling crowd at the corner where he normally sat. He said authoritatively, 'Leave way, please.' But no one cared. It was the young shop-boy of the stationer's that plucked his sleeve and said, 'They have been fighting over something since the evening. . . .'

'Over what?' asked Rama.

'Over something . . .' the boy said. 'People say someone was stabbed near the Sales Tax Office when he was distributing notices about some votes or something. It may be a private quarrel. But who cares? Let them fight who want a fight.'

Someone said, 'How dare you speak like that about us?'

Everyone turned to look at this man sourly. Someone in that crowd remarked, 'Can't a man speak . . . ?'

His neighbour slapped him for it. Rama stood there with his load about him, looking on helplessly. This one slap was enough to set off a fuse. Another man hit another man and then another hit another, and someone started a cry, 'Down with. . . .'

'Ah, it is as we suspected, pre-planned and organized to crush us . . .' another section cried.

People shouted, soda-water bottles were used as missiles. Everyone hit everyone else. A set of persons suddenly entered all the shops and demanded that these be closed. 'Why?' asked the shopmen. 'How can you have the heart to do business when . . . ?'

The restraints of civilized existence were suddenly abandoned. Everyone seemed to be angry with everyone else. Within an hour the whole scene looked like a battlefield. Of course the police came on to the spot presently, but this made matters worse, since it provided another side to the fight. The police had a three-fold task, of maintaining law and order and also maintaining themselves intact and protecting some party whom they believed to be injured. Shops that were not closed were looted.

The cinema house suddenly emptied itself of its crowd, which rushed out to enter the fray at various points. People with knives ran about, people with blood-stains groaned and shouted, ambulance vans moved here and there. The police used lathis and tear-gas, and finally opened fire. Many people died. The public said that the casualties were three thousand, but the official communiqué maintained that only five were injured and four-and-a-quarter killed in the police firing. At midnight Rama emerged from his hiding place under a culvert and went home.

The next day Rama told his wife, 'I won't take out the usual quantity. I doubt if there will be anyone there. God knows what devil has seized all those folk! They are ready to kill each other for some votes. . . .' His instinct was right. There were more policemen than public on Market Road and his corner was strongly guarded. He had to set up his shop on a farther spot indicated by a police officer.

Matters returned to normal in about ten days, when all the papers clamoured for a full public enquiry into this or that: whether the firing was justified and what precautions were taken by the police to prevent this flare-up and so on. Rama watched the unfolding of contemporary history through the shouts of news-boys, and in due course tried to return to his corner. The moment he set up his tray and took his seat, a couple of young men wearing badges came to him and said: 'You can't have your shop here.'

'Why not, sir?'

'This is a holy spot on which our leader fell that day. The police aimed their guns at his heart. We are erecting a monument here. This is our place; the municipality have handed this corner to us.'

Very soon this spot was cordoned off, with some congregation or the other always there. Money boxes jingled for collections and people dropped coins. Rama knew better than anyone else how good the place was for attracting money. They collected enough money to set up a memorial stone and, with an ornamental fencing and flowerpots, entirely transformed the spot.

Austere, serious-looking persons arrived there and spoke among themselves. Rama had to move nearly two hundred yards away, far into the lane. It meant that he went out of the range of vision of his customers. He fell on their blind-spot. The cinema crowd emerging from the theatre poured away from him; the jutka-drivers who generally left their vehicles on the roadside for a moment while the traffic constable showed indulgence and snatched a mouthful, found it inconvenient to come so far; the boot-boys patronized a fellow on the opposite foot-path, the scraggy pretender, whose fortunes seemed to be rising.

Nowadays Rama prepared very much less stock each day, but even then he carried home a lot of remnants. He consumed some of these at home, and the rest, on his wife's advice, he warmed up and brought out for sale again next day. One or two who tasted the stuff retched and spread the rumour that Rama's quality was not what it used to be. One night, when he went home with just two annas in his bag, he sat up on the pyol and announced to his wife, 'I believe our business is finished. Let us not think of it any more.'

He put away his pans and trays and his lamp, and prepared himself for a life of retirement. When all his savings were exhausted he went to one Restaurant Kohinoor from which loudspeakers shrieked all day, and queued up for a job. For twenty rupees a month he waited eight hours a day at the tables. People came and went, the radio music from somewhere frayed his nerves, but he stuck on; he had to. When some customer ordered him about too rudely, he said, 'Gently, brother. I was once a hotel-owner myself.' And with that piece of reminiscence he attained great satisfaction.

From *Lawley Road and Other Stories*, 1956

Dasi the Bridegroom

His name was Dasi. In all the Extension there was none like him—an uncouth fellow with a narrow tapering head, bulging eyes, and fat neck; below the neck he had an immense body, all muscle. God had not endowed him with very fluent speech. He gurgled and lisped like an infant. His age was a mystery. It might be anything between twenty and fifty. He lived in a house in the last street. It was a matter of perpetual speculation how he was related to the master of the house. Some persons said he was a younger brother, and some said he had been a foundling brought up by the gentleman. Whatever it was it was not a matter which could be cleared by Dasi himself—for, as I have already said, he could not even say how old he was. If you asked, he said a hundred one day and five on the next. In return for the food and protection he received, he served the family in his own way; he drew water from the well from dawn till mid-day, chopped wood, and dug the garden.

Dasi went out in the afternoon. When he stepped out scores of children followed him about shouting and jeering. Hawkers and passers-by stopped to crack a joke at his expense. There was particularly a group in a house nicknamed *Mantapam*. In the front porch of the house were gathered all day a good company of old men; persons who had done useful work in their time but who now found absolutely nothing to do at any part of the day. They were ever on the look out for some excitement or gossip. To them Dasi was a source of great joy. The moment Dasi was sighted they would shout, 'Hey, fellow, have you fixed up a bride?' This question never failed to draw Dasi in, for he thought very deeply and earnestly of his marriage. When he came and squatted in their midst on the floor they would say, 'The marriage season is closing, you must hurry up, my dear fellow.'

'Yes, yes,' Dasi would reply. 'I am going to the priest. He has promised to settle it today.'

'Today?'

'Yes, tonight I am going to be married. They said so.'

'Who?'

'My uncle. . . .'

'Who is your uncle?'

'My elder brother is my uncle. I am in his house and draw water from his well. See how my hand is . . . all the skin is gone. . . .' He would spread out his fingers and show his palms. They would feel his palms and say, 'Hardened like wood! Poor fellow! This won't do, my dear fellow, you must quickly marry and put an end to all this . . .' Dasi's eyes would brighten at this suggestion, and his lips would part in a happy smile showing an enormous front tooth. Everyone would laugh at it, and he too would sway and rock with laughter.

And then the question, 'Where is your bride?'

'She is there . . . in Madras . . . in Madras. . . .'

'What is she like?'

'She has eyes like this,' said Dasi, and drew a large circle in the air with his finger.

'What is the colour of her skin?'

'Very, very white.'

'Has she long hair?'

Dasi indicated an immense flow of tresses with his hand.

'Is she very good looking?'

'She is . . . yes, yes.'

Dasi hid his face in his hand, looked at the group through a corner of his eye and said shyly, 'Yes, yes, I also like her.'

'Where have you the money to marry?'

'They have to give me three thousand rupees,' replied Dasi.

'He means that his wages have accumulated,' some one explained obligingly.

When he went home he was asked where he had been and he said, 'My marriage.' And then he went and sat down in the shed on his mat, his only possession in the world. He remained there brooding over his marriage till he was called in to dine, late in the night. He was the last to eat because he consumed an immense quantity of rice, and they thought it a risk to call him in before the others had eaten. After food he carried huge cauldrons of water and washed the kitchen and dining-hall floor. And then he went to his mat and slept till dawn, when he woke up and drew water from the well.

For years out of count this had been going on. Even his life had a tone and rhythm of its own. He never seemed to long for anything or interfere in anybody's business; never spoke to others except when spoken to; never so much as thought he was being joked at; he treated everyone seriously; when the Extension School children ran behind him jeering he never even showed he was aware of their presence; he had no doubt the strength of an ox, but he had also the forbearance of Mother Earth; nothing ever seemed to irritate him. . . .

The little cottage in the third street which had remained vacant from time immemorial suddenly shed its 'To Let' notice. Along with the newspaper and the letters, the train one morning brought a film star from Madras, called Bamini Bai—a young person all smiles, silk and powder. She took up her abode in the little cottage.

Very soon the Extension folk knew all about her. She was going to stay in Malgudi a considerable time training herself under a famous musician of the town. She had her old mother staying with her. The Extension folk had also a complete knowledge of her movements. She left home early in the morning, returned at midday, slept till three o'clock, went out on a walk along the Trunk Road at five o'clock, and so on.

At the Mantapam they told Dasi one day, 'Dasi, your wife has arrived.'

'Where?' asked Dasi. He became agitated, and swallowed and struggled to express all the anxiety and happiness he felt. The company assumed a very serious expression and said, 'Do you know the house in the next street, the little house . . . ?'

'Yes, yes.'

'She is there. Have you not seen her?'

Dasi hid his face in his hands and went away. He went to the next street. It was about one o'clock in the afternoon. The film star was not to be seen. Dasi stood on the road looking at the house for some time. He returned to the Mantapam. They greeted him vociferously. 'How do you like her?' Dasi replied, 'My eyes did not see her, the door would not open.'

'Try to look in through the window. You will see her.'

'I will see through the window,' said Dasi, and started out again.

'No, no, stop. It is no good. Listen to me. Will you do as I say?'

'Yes, yes.'

'You see, she goes out every day at five o'clock. You will see her if you go to Trichy Road and wait.'

Dasi's head was bowed in shyness. They goaded him on, and he went along to the Trunk Road and waited. He sat under a tree on the roadside. It was not even two o'clock, and he had to wait till nearly six. The sun beat down fully on his face. He sat leaning against a tree trunk and brooded. A few cars passed raising dust, bullock carts with jingling bells, and villagers were moving about the highway; but Dasi saw nothing and noticed nothing. He sat looking down the road. And after all she came along. Dasi's throat went dry at the sight of her. His temples throbbed, and sweat stood out on his brow. He had never seen anything like her in all his life. The vision of beauty and youth dazzled him. He was confused and bewildered. He sprang on to his feet and ran home at full speed. He lay down on his mat in the shed. He was so much absorbed in his thoughts that he wouldn't get up when they called him in to dinner. His master walked to the shed and shook him up. 'What is the matter with you?' he asked.

'My marriage. . . . She is there. She is all right.'

'Well, well. Go and eat and do your work, you fool,' said his master.

Next afternoon Dasi was again at the Trunk Road. This became his daily habit. Every day his courage increased. At last came a day when he could stare at her. His face relaxed and his lips parted in a smile when she passed him, but that young lady had other thoughts to occupy her mind and did not notice him. He waited till she returned that way and tried to smile at her again, though it was nearly dark and she was looking away. He followed her, his face lit up with joy. She opened the gate of her cottage and walked in. He hesitated a moment, and followed her in. He stood under the electric lamp in the hall. The mother came out of the kitchen and asked Dasi, 'Who are you?'

Dasi looked at her and smiled; at that the old lady was frightened. She cried, 'Bama, who is this man in the hall?' Bamini Bai came out of her room. 'Who are you?' she asked. Dasi melted at the sight of her. Even the little expression he was capable of left him. He blinked and gulped and looked suffocated. His eyes blazed forth love. His lips struggled to smile. With great difficulty he said, 'Wife . . . wife, you are the wife. . . .'

'What are you saying?'

'You are my wife,' he repeated, and moved nearer. She recoiled with horror, and struck him in the face. And then she and her mother set up such a cry that all the neighbours and passers-by rushed in. Somebody brought in a police Sub-Inspector. Dasi was marched off to the police station. The members of the Mantapam used their influence and had him released late in the night. He went home and lay on his mat. His body had received numerous blows from all sorts of people in the evening; but he hardly felt or remembered any of them. But his soul revolted against the memory of the slap he had received in the face. . . . When they called him in to eat, he refused to get up. His master went to him and commanded, 'Go and eat, Dasi. You are bringing me disgrace, you fool. Don't go out of the house hereafter.' Dasi refused to get up. He rolled himself in the mat and said, 'Go, I don't eat.' He turned and faced the wall.

On the following day Dasi had the misfortune to step out of his house just when the children of the Elementary School were streaming out at midday interval. They had heard all about the incident of the previous evening. They now surrounded him and cried, 'Hey, bridegroom.' He turned and looked at them; there were tears in his eyes. He made a gesture of despair and appealed to them: 'Go, go, don't trouble me. . . . Go.'

'Oh, the bridegroom is still crying; his wife beat him yesterday,' said a boy. On hearing this Dasi let out a roar, lifted the boy by his collar and hurled him into the crowd. He swung his arms about and knocked down people who tried to get near him. He rushed into the school and broke chairs and tables. He knocked down four teachers who tried to restrain him. He rushed out of the school and assaulted everyone he met. He crashed into the shops and threw things about. He leapt about like a panther from place to place; he passed through the streets of the Extension like a tornado. . . .

Gates were hurriedly shut and bolted. A group of persons tried to run behind Dasi, while a majority preferred to take cover. Soon the police were on the scene, and Dasi was finally overpowered.

He was kept that night in a police lock-up, and sent to the Mental Hospital next day. He was not very easy to manage at first. He was kept in a cell for some weeks. He begged the doctor one day to allow him to stand at the main gate and look down the road. The doctor promised this as a reward for good behaviour. Dasi valued the reward so much that he did everything everyone suggested for a whole week. He was then sent (with a warder) to the main gate where he stood for a whole hour looking down the road for the coming of his bride.

From *An Astrologer's Day
and Other Stories*, 1947

RAJA RAO

Raja Rao was born at Hassan, Karnataka, in 1909 in a Brahmin family and went to school in Hyderabad. Later, after studying French at Aligarh Muslim University, he graduated from Nizam College, Hyderabad. He also studied at the Universities of Montpellier and the Sorbonne. His first novel, *Kanthapura*, appeared in 1938. This was followed by *The Serpent and the Rope* (1960) which won him the Sahitya Akademi Award in 1964. His other works include *The Cat and Shakespeare* (1965) and *Comrade Kirillov* (1976). His short stories have been collected in *The Cow of the Barricades* (1947) and *The Policeman and the Rose* (1978).

In the author's 'Foreword' to *Kanthapura*, Raja Rao observes that 'tempo' is the most characteristic element of the Indian mode of consciousness. 'We, in India, think quickly, we talk quickly, and when we move we move quickly.' This is borne out admirably in 'The True Story of Kanakapala'. Narrated by Old Venkamma, Plantation Subbayya's sick mother, this story rambles on like a folk-tale and conjures up a world of superstition and faith in which Kanakapala, 'a huge three-striped cobra', acts as the dispenser of justice, protector of the virtuous and enemy of the wicked. It should be interesting to compare Khushwant Singh's 'The Mark of Vishnu' and Raja Rao's 'The True Story of Kanakapala' to understand how the snake often emerges in Indian fiction as a multifaceted symbol.

'Javni' deals with the perennial theme of universal fellowship that brooks no barriers of caste, colour or creed. The quotation from Kanakadas that heads the story aptly epitomizes its essence: 'What caste, pray, has he who knows God?' 'Javni' is a story of love and hate—and of suffering that always moulds us into the true image of God. Ramappa recognizes the spark of true divinity in Javni, the wretched widow of low caste who, slighted and humiliated by her kith and kin, emerges as a symbol of faith, endurance and compassion. Touched by the nobility of her soul, Ramappa, a Brahmin, offers to be adopted by her. To his sister Sita, he exclaims, 'Are they not like us, like any of us?' 'Javni', like many of Raja Rao's stories, is also written in a racy style that represents the 'tempo' of the Indian mode of living and talking.

The True Story of Kanakapala, Protector of Gold

The serpent is a friend or an enemy. If he is a friend, he lives with you, guarding your riches, protecting your health, and making you holy, and if he is an enemy, he slips through the kitchen gutter or through the granary tiles, or better still through the byre's eaves, and rushing towards you, he spreads his hood and *bhoos*, he flings himself at you, and if he is a quarter-of-an-hour one, you die in a quarter of an hour, a three-fourths-of-an-hour one, you die in three-fourths of an hour, and you may know it by the number of stripes he has on his hood, for one means a quarter of an hour, two half an hour, and three three-fourths, but beyond that you can never live; unless of course there is a barber in the village who is so learned in the mysteries of animal wisdom that he stands near, a jug of water in one hand and a cup of milk in the other, chanting weird things in hoarse voices, with strange contortions of the face; and then Lord Naga slips through the gutter, tiles or eaves, exactly as he went out, and coming near the barber like a whining dog before its frenzied master, touches the wounded man at exactly the spot where he has injected his venom, and sucking back the poison, spits it into the milk-cup, and like a dog too, slowly first, timidly, hushed, he creeps over the floor, and the further he goes the greater he takes strength, and when he is near the door, suddenly doubles his speed and slips away—never to be seen again. The barber is paid three rupees, a shawl, and coconut with betel-leaves, and, for you, a happy life with your wife and children, not to speak of the studied care of an attentive mother-in-law, and the fitful grumblings of that widow of a sister who does not show even a wink of gratitude for all your kindness.

But, never mind, for the important thing is that you are alive. May you live a thousand years!

But the story I'm going to tell you is the story of a serpent when he is a friend. It was recounted to me one monsoon evening last June, by old Venkamma, Plantation Subbayya's sick mother. May those who read this be beloved of Naga, King of Serpents, Destroyer of Ills.

Vision Rangappa, the first member of the family, belonged to Hosur near Mysore, and was of humble parents. His father and mother had died when he was hardly a boy of eighteen, and being left alone he accepted to be a pontifical brahmin— the only job for one in his condition. People liked his simple nature, the deference in his movements, and the deep gravity of his voice; and whenever there were festivals or obsequies to be performed, they invited him to dinner. And when he had duly honoured them with his brahmanic presence, and partaken of the holy meal, they gave him half an anna and a coconut, for his pontifical services. But nobody ever suspected that the money was never used, and that it went straight into a sacred copper pot, sealed with wax at the top, and with a slit in the lid. Six pies a week, or sometimes one anna a week, could become a large amount some day. For he secretly hoped that one auspicious morning he would leave this village and start towards Kashi, on pilgrimage. That was the reason why he had refused bride after bride, some beautiful as new-opened guavas, and others tender as April mangoes, and some too with dowries that could buy over a kingdom. 'No,' he would tell himself, 'not till I have seen the beautiful Kashi-Vishweshwara with my own eyes. Once I have had that vision, I will wed a holy wife and live among my children and children's children.' Thus resolved, every day he calculated how much money there would be in the holy pot—it would be a sin to open it!— and every day he said to himself that in one year, in nine months, in six months, in three months, or maybe in two fortnights, he would leave this little village and start off on his great pilgrimage.

And it so happened, that there was a sudden epidemic which

swept across the whole country, and nearly every house had
one or two that disappeared into the realm of Brahma. So,
Hosakere Rangappa—who was not yet Vision Rangappa—
made nearly ten times the money in less than a month, and
besides, as three rich families offered him a cow each in honour
of the departed spirits, he determined to sell them back and
pour gold into the holy pot. 'What shall I do with these cattle?'
he explained to the donors, 'I have neither field nor byre. I
pray you, imagine you have given them to me, and pay me in
return whatever gold you may think fit.' And they paid him
in pies of copper, rupees of silver, and mohurs of gold, and he
put the copper and the silver and the gold into the holy pot. He
lifted it up. It weighed enormously. It weighed as though there
was nothing but solid gold in it. He went into the village temple,
fell prostrate before the gods, and having asked the blessings of
the whole village—who offered him again half an anna each to
honour him—he left the village under a propitious star, when
the sun was touching the middle of the temple spire. He was
happy, he was going to Kashi. He would bathe in the Ganges
and have the supreme vision of Kashi-Vishweshwara. And then,
purified of all sin, he would return home a holy man. They
would receive him with conchs and trumpets, and with a gold-
bordered parasol. . . . And as he walked along the road, all
things seemed to wake up and weep that they too could not go
along to Kashi with him. People passing in bullock carts—for
there were no trains then—stopped and fell at his feet on seeing
him garmented as one who goes to Kashi. They gave him
rice and money, and some even gave him clothes. And thus
Rangappa went from village to village, from town to town,
towards the holy city of Kashi.

One day he arrived on the sparkling banks of the Hemavathy.
He had his bath, did his evening meditation, and having drunk
three handfuls of water, he went into the serai to sleep. And
as he lay down he saw before him a bare, rocky hill, and the
moonlight poured over it like a milk and butter libation. He
was so overcome with fatigue that sleep crept gently over him.
In the middle of the night he saw in his dream a beautiful

vision. Kashi-Vishweshwara and his Holy Companion stood above his head, and spoke thus: 'We have been touched by your indestructible devotion, and we show ourselves unto you that you may be protected from the blisters of pilgrim proddings and the pinches of the weary spirit. You are sanctified by our holy presence. Your pilgrimage is now over. But on the top of the hill before you there raise unto us a temple that we may sprout through the earth and live for ever amidst unfailing worship. Your duty is to look after the temple, and generation after generation of your family will be beloved of us. May our blessings be on you.' And the Holy Couple were lost through a choir of clouds.

The next morning when Rangappa had duly taken his bath in the river and had said his prayers, he went up the hill, feeling purified and exalted. On a rock at the very top, he saw the figure of Shiva as linga and Parvathi with her holy tress and crown, as though carved but yesternight, and yet how old, and shapeful and serene. He sat beside the Udbhavamurti, and meditated for twenty-one days without food, fruit or water. A shepherd boy discovered him, and rushing to the town cried out from end to end of the streets that a holy man had sat himself on the top of the hill in rapt meditation. People came with fruits and flowers and with many sweetly perfumed preparations of rice, pulses and flour, and placing them before him, begged of him to honour the humble ones with his blessings. He spoke unto them of his vision, and each one hurried down the hill and ran up back to the summit, bringing copper plates and silver plates and golden plates, and placed them before him. He touched the offerings, and asked them to build the temple. Four walls of stone rose above the rock before the sun had set, and Hosakere Rangappa—now become Vision Rangappa— sanctified the temple with hymns from the *Atharva-veda*. And the holy pot stood by the Holy Couple. It belonged to them.

The whole town rejoiced that Kashi-Vishweshwara and his Divine Companion had honoured their poor Subbehalli with their permanent presence. They gave dinners and organized processions, and renamed their village Kashipura. Vision Rangappa married the third daughter of Pandit Sivaramayya, and settled down in the village. And for fear the armies of the redman, which were battling then with the Sultan of Mysore, should rob them of the moneypot, he brought it home and, digging a hole beneath the family sanctum, put it there, and covered it over with mud and stone.

The next day, a huge three-striped cobra, with eyes like sapphire, and the jewel in the hood, lay curled upon the spot, for the cobra is the eternal guardian of sacred gold. And they called him Kanakapala—protector of gold.

Over a hundred years have now passed, and things have changed in Kashipura as all over the world. People have grown from boys to young men, from young men to men with children, and then to aged grandfathers, and some too have left for the woods to meditate, and others have died a common death, surrounded by wife and children, and children's children. Others have become rich, after having begged in the streets; while some have become villains, though they were once the gentlest of the meek. And some—Shiva forgive them!—are lying eaten by disease though they were strong as bulls and pious as dedicated cows. Those who have become rich have children, those who have become wicked have children, and those who have become sick may have had children too, and after a hundred years, their children's children are living to still see the Hemavathy hurl herself against the elephant-headed rock, and churning round the Harihara hills—just beneath the temple—leap forth into the breathful valleys, amidst gardens of mango and coconut, rice and sugarcane. Three times, they say, the Goddess Hemavathy has grown so furious with the sins of her children, that she has risen in tempestuous rage, and swelling like a demon, swept away the trees, the crops, and the cattle— leaving behind sands where there was soil fine as powder of gold, and rock and stone where the mangoes stretched down as though to rest themselves on the soft green earth below. Coconut trees too were uprooted, and at least three houses were washed away, roofs and all . . . but that was some fifteen years ago—the last flood. Since then nothing very important has happened in

Kashipura, unless of course you count among big events the untimely death of the old Eight-verandahed-house Chowdayya, the third marriage of the old widower Cardamom-field Venkatesha, the sale of Tippayya's mango garden, the elopement of Sidda's daughter, Kenchi, with the Revenue Inspector's servant. But—and here, as Old Venkamma told me the story, she grew more and more animated—'the biggest event without doubt is the one I am going to tell you about, of how the Vision-House brothers, Surappa, the eldest, and Ranganna, the third brother—pushed, as they say, though nobody knows the entire truth to this day—pushed their second brother Seetharamu into the river—you know why? . . . to have gold . . . to have the gold of Kanakapala. Nobody speaks loudly of it, but who does not know they have drowned him? You had only to see, how of late Kanakapala, who even when you accidentally put your foot on him lay quiet as a lamb, now spreads his hood, as soon as he discovers you, and was even heard to pursue the carpenter Ranga to the door. After all, my son, if Kanakapala did not know of it, who else could have discovered it, tell me? Of course I do not know the story. But this is what they say. Now listen!

'You know, in the Vision-House, since the good old father Ramakrishnayya died, they had been trying to murder one another. Oh! to have had a father with a heart pure as the morning lotus, so pious, so generous, and venerable as a saint, that such a father should have children like this! Shiva, Shiva, bestow unto us Thy light! Well, after all, my son, who can save us from our karma? It was perhaps his karma to see his children turn base as pariahs, and quarrel like street-dogs. Of course as long as he lived, they never fought openly. They beat each other in the garden, or when the father had gone to the temple; and when they saw Ramakrishnayya they suddenly changed into calves, so mild, so soft, and so deferent. Once he caught Surappa the elder, and Ranganna the third—the same who were to commit the horrid deed—he caught them pulling the branch of the champak tree, when Seetharamu had gone up to pluck flowers for the morning worship. "What are you up to?" Ramakrishnayya cried. "Nothing! Nothing!" they answered, and stood trembling before him. "We are just going to play Hopping-monkey." "Hopping-monkey! Why not have four more children, you pariahs, before playing Hopping-monkey!" For, you must remember, at that time Surappa was twenty-six, married and had already two children, and Ranganna had just come back after his nuptials. Seetharamu had lost his wife in that horrible malarial fever, and was just intending to marry again. That happened when our little Ramu was going through his initiation ceremony—that is, some four years to next Dassera. Since that day, the father is supposed to have taken great care of Seetharamu, for he loved him the most—learned and obedient and respectful as he was—and he often took him to the temple, lest the worst happen at home. Good Ranganayakamma, Rama-krishnayya's sister, was pretty old, and had for long been blind, and nobody would listen to her now. Of course, there was Sata, the widowed daughter, who could easily have taken care of Seetharamu. But, she herself, as every woman in this village knows, was greedy, malicious, and clever as a jackal. They even said she had poisoned her husband because he was too old for her, and take my word, she was malignant minx enough to do it. Anyway, since she came back home, she has been more with Surappa, and Ranganna, than with Seetharamu. I wonder if everybody believes in it. Never, however, speak of it to anyone, my child, will you? But everybody says, the very first day she came home, she discovered how things were going there, and tried to poison Seetharamu. She even did poison him, they say, for, if you remember, he fell seriously ill soon after her arrival, and vomited nothing but blood—red blood, black blood and violet blood; and it was during that same week too we saw Kanakapala furious for the first time, and lying near Seeth-aramu's bed, to guard him from further harm. How he lay there, quiet and awake, eyes shining like jewels, and the old, old skin dandruff-covered and parched, shrivelled like the cast-off skin of a plantain. Somehow Kanakapala had an especial love for Seetharamu. When he was born, they say Kanakapala had slowly slipped into the room, and stealing into the cradle, had spread his hood over the child, and disappeared with the swiftness of lightning. No wonder Seetharamu was such a godlike boy. He must have been one of the chosen ones. He was always so smiling, so serene, so full of respect and affection. Why, if I had a daughter to marry, I would have given her away to him! Anyway, he married a good girl, and it is unfortunate she died before bearing him a child. It *is* so unfortunate. . . .

'However, to come back to the story. Surappa and Ranganna wanted somehow to kill Seetharamu, because they knew he would never think of digging out that gold their ancestors had offered to the gods. By the way, my son, do you know what they say about it? First, it was under the sanctum. Then it moved—under the earth of course!—to the dining room, then later to the granary, and lastly it was under the lumber-room by the kitchen. Not that anyone knows about it, for sure. But wherever the serpent sleeps is *the* spot. If not, why should Kanakapala change place so often? And why does he not sleep always in the same place, once he has chosen his abode? Gold, you know, moves about from place to place lest the wicked find it. Only the holy ones can touch it. Seetharamu alone could go to the lumber-room, for Kanakapala knew the true from the false, as the rat knows the grain from the husk. Once, it was said, Surappa actually entered the lumber-room when Kanakapala was being fed with milk by Sata, and somehow—for the snakes have understanding where we human beings do not have—he knew of it, and spitting back the milk into the cup rushed to the spot, and having spread his hood hissed and bellowed and bit Surappa, without of course injecting any venom, for being of the temple it can never sting a Vision-House man. He yelled and ran into the kitchen. "What is it?" cried Seetharamu, running to his brother's rescue.

' "Nothing, nothing at all. When I was passing by the lumber-room, Kanakapala pursued me, though I'd done nothing. Perhaps he was just chasing his prey. . . ."

'Seetharamu hurried to the lumber-room, scolded Kanakapala angrily; and the poor fellow lay there quiet, curled and flat, and with wide-open eyes. He seemed tame as a dog. Since then Kanakapala has never pursued anybody. Somehow Seeth-

aramu seemed to have commanded him not to. Oh! that
he should have faith in these people! But, my son, who can
imagine that your own brothers are going to murder you so
that they may have the money—and holy money too!—holy
money that your grandfathers have offered to the gods? ...
Well, but the world is changing. We are living in Kali Yuga.
And don't they say, for every million virtuous men there were
in the first Yuga, every thousand in the second, every hundred
in the third, there is but one now? Unrighteousness becomes the
master, and virtue is being trodden down. Oh, when our grandfathers were alive, how happily we lived. We bought a khanda
of rice for half a rupee, and seven seers of ghee for a rupee. And
now.... You must beat your mouth and yell.... Oh, to live
in this poor, polluted world....

'Anyway Ramakrishnayya died. You know Kanakapala lay
by his corpse till they took him away. And when they had lifted
up the corpse, Kanakapala spat out poison once, twice, thrice.
... That was how he showed his grief. And he never touched
milk for three full days. Such was Kanakapala!

'A week later the three brothers had begun to quarrel about
the division of property. Each one said—though it is impossible
to believe that Seetharamu could have said it—that he wanted
the mango garden. They could not agree over it. First it was
Surappa and Ranganna that had growled at each other. And
when Seetharamu simply said: "Why quarrel over such small
things?" they both fell upon him—it must surely have been
planned out—and beat him on the stomach and on the back.
The old blind aunt went into the kitchen, and Sata ran about
the house, pretending to cry and sob. That widow to sob! If she
had a lover in her bed, she would not sob, hé? And nobody
came to separate the fighting brothers. It was Kanakapala, who,
strange to say, suddenly appeared and, slipping between the
two aggressors and Seetharamu, tried to separate them. But
when they continued he roped himself round the foot of Surappa
who staggered and fell. Then Kanakapala frightened Ranganna
with his spread hood, and Ranganna ran out breathlessly....
And Seetharamu lay on the floor, quiet, blank-eyed, and with

no evil in his heart, while Kanakapala gently moved his tail about his face in friendly caress.

'That was as you know the last quarrel they had at home. It was hardly a fortnight later that Seetharamu's body was discovered in the Hemavathy. As to how it happened, everybody has his own opinion about it. My own is slightly different from that of others, because being their neighbour, and third cousin, I have more reasons to know these things than most people. Besides, I am an old woman, and I have seen so many domestic calamities that I can quite surmise how this could have happened too. Listen.

'Now, you will perhaps call me wicked, maybe I am wicked. But tell me, how else can one explain the sudden death of Seetharamu if not by realizing that his two brothers hated him and, wanting the gold, drowned him in the river? Of course, people will tell you they were both lying sick at home, and nobody knows how Seetharamu, who went to Kanthapura to look after the peasants that were going to sow rice, should suddenly have disappeared. There is the boatman, Sidda. You know how at least two murders—of Dasappa of the oil-shop, and Sundrappa of the stream-fed-field—in both of them he was implicated. You know too how he beats his wife, and no child will ever approach him. Now, Sidda was to ply Seetharamu across the river, for the field lay on the Kanthapura side, and he says he never saw Seetharamu. If he had not seen Seetharamu, who else could have seen him, tell me? I myself saw Seetharamu passing by our door. And when I asked him where he was going, he told me clearly that he was going to Kanthapura to look after the sowings, as the two brothers were sick. Sick! I know what that sickness was! They looked hale and strong as exhibition bulls. They must simply have starved themselves to bear a pale face two days later. The evening before they were quite well, and if Big-House Subbayya is to be believed, they were talking to Sidda, a long, long time. The case is plain. Sidda pushed Seetharamu into the river. Any honest person in the village will believe it. But they are afraid of the Vision-House people. Besides they want to have nothing to do with the police.

And who does not know the Police Inspector has been duly bribed by them? I have myself seen the Police Inspector, a fat, vicious, green-looking brute, staying day after day in the Vision-House. . . . But nobody will accept this version. Maybe I am wicked. May God forgive me for my tongue! But, if I had no children, I will tell you what I would do, my son: I would poison these two brothers, and, drinking half a seer of warm milk with undisturbed contentment, I would go and drown myself in the river, happy . . . very happy.

'Poor Seetharamu!

'After that the story is simple. One day when Sata kept feeding Kanakapala in the kitchen, the two brothers closed the sanctum door and began to dig. Kanakapala swung out and hurled his head against the door, hissing and rasping. But there was no answer. Furious he ran to the roof, and slipped into the eaves, but every chink and hole had been closed with cloth and coconut rind. He rushed back to the kitchen again but there was no one. He ran to the byre, spitting venom at every breath . . . and there was no one. Then, frantic, helpless, repentant, he rushed out of the door and scampered up the hill. Entering the temple, he went round and round the god and goddess, once, twice, thrice, and curling himself at the foot of the Divine Couple, swallowed his tail, and died. For is it not said, a snake loves death better than an undutiful life?

'The Vision-House people never found the gold. But with what libations have they now to wash away their sins! Child after child, new-born child, new-lisping child, new-walking child, young child, old child, school-going child, have met with mysterious, untimely deaths. And no woman in their family can ever bear a child for nine months and bring it forth, for the malediction of Naga is upon them. Never, never till seven times are they dead, and seven times are they reborn, can they wear out their sacrilegious act. . . . Oh, sinners, sinners!

'And to this day there is not a woman, child or man in Kashipura that has not heard the money clinking in the earth, for holy gold moves from place to place, lest the wicked find it. And that same night Kanakapala appears in the dream of woman, child or man, frantic, helpless, repentant and scampering up the hill, goes round the god and goddess, once, twice, thrice, and curling himself at the foot of the Divine Couple, swallows his tail—and dies.'

I too have dreamt of it, believe me—else I wouldn't have written this story.

From *The Cow of the Barricades and Other Stories*, 1947

Javni

Caste and caste and caste, you say,
What caste, pray, has he who knows God?
                            —KANAKADAS

I had just arrived. My sister sat by me, talking to me about a thousand things—about my health, my studies, my future, about Mysore, about my younger sister—and I lay sipping the hot, hot coffee that seemed almost like nectar after a ten-mile cycle ride on one of those bare, dusty roads of Malkad. I half listened to her and half drowsed away, feeling comfort and freedom after nine wild months in a city. And when I finished my coffee, I asked my sister to go and get another cup; for I really felt like being alone, and also I wanted some more of that invigorating drink. When my sister was gone, I lay on the mat, flat on my face with my hands stretched at my sides. It seemed to me I was carried away by a flood of some sort, caressing, feathery and quiet. I slept. Suddenly, as if in a dream, I heard a door behind me creaking. But I did not move. The door did not open completely, and somebody seemed to be standing by the threshold afraid to come in. 'Perhaps a neighbour,' I said to myself vaguely, and in my drowsiness I muttered something, stretched out my hands, kicked my feet against the floor and slowly moved my head from one side to the other. The door creaked a little again, and the figure seemed to recede. 'Lost!' I said to myself. Perhaps I had sent a neighbour away. I was a little pained. But some deeper instinct told me that the figure was still there. Outside the carts rumbled over the paved street, and some crows cawed across the roof. A few sunbeams stealing through the tiles fell upon my back. I felt happy.

Meanwhile my sister came in, bringing the coffee. 'Ramu,' she whispered, standing by me, 'Ramu, my child, are you awake or asleep?'

'Awake,' I said, turning my head towards the door, which creaked once more and shut itself completely.

'Sita,' I whispered, 'there was somebody at the door.'

'When?' she demanded loudly.

'Now! Only a moment ago.'

She went to the door and, opening it, looked towards the street. After a while she smiled and called, 'Javni! You monkey! Why don't you come in? Who do you think is here, Javni? My brother—my brother.' She smiled broadly, and a few tears rolled down her cheeks.

'Really, Mother!' said a timid voice. 'Really! I wanted to come in. But, seeing Ramappa fast asleep, I thought I'd better wait out here.' She spoke the peasant Kannada, drawling the vowels interminably.

'So,' I said to myself, 'she already knows my name.'

'Come in!' commanded my sister.

Javni slowly approached the threshold, but still stood outside, gazing as if I were a saint or the holy elephant.

'Don't be shy, come in,' commanded my sister again.

Javni entered and, walking as if in a temple, went and sat by a sack of rice.

My sister sat by me, proud and affectionate. I was everything to her—her strength and wealth. She touched my head and said, 'Ramu, Javni is our new servant.' I turned towards Javni. She seemed to hide her face.

She was past forty, a little wrinkled beneath the lips and with strange, rapturous eyes. Her hair was turning white, her breasts were fallen and her bare, broad forehead showed pain and widowhood. 'Come near, Javni,' I said.

'No, Ramappa,' she whispered.

'No, come along,' I insisted. She came forward a few steps and sat by the pillar.

'Oh, come nearer, Javni, and see what a beautiful brother I have,' cried Sita.

I was not flattered. Only my big, taplike nose and my thick underlip seemed more monstrous than ever.

Javni crawled along till she was a few steps nearer.

'Oh! come nearer, you monkey,' cried my sister again.

Javni advanced a few feet further and, turning her face towards the floor, sat like a bride beside the bridegroom.

'He looks a prince, Javni!' cried my sister.

'A god!' mumbled Javni.

I laughed and drank my coffee.

'The whole town is mad about him,' whispered Javni.

'How do you know?' asked Sita.

'How! I have been standing at the market-place, the whole afternoon, to see when Ramappa would come. You told me he looked like a prince. You said he rode a bicycle. And, when I saw him come by the pipal tree where-the-fisherman-Kodi-hanged-himself-the-other-day, I ran towards the town and I observed how people gazed and gazed at him. And they asked me who it was. "Of course, the Revenue Inspector's brother-in-law," I replied. "How beautiful he is!" said fat Nanjundah of the coconut shop. "How like a prince he is!" said the concubine Chowdy. "Oh, a very god!" said my neighbour, barber Venka's wife Kenchi.'

'Well, Ramu, so you see, the whole of Malkad is dazzled with your beauty,' interrupted my sister. 'Take care, my child. They say, in this town they practise magic, and I have heard many a beautiful boy has been killed by jealousy.'

I laughed.

'Don't laugh, Ramappa. With these very eyes, with these very two eyes, I have seen the ghosts of more than a hundred young men and women—all killed by magic, by magic, Ramappa,' assured Javni, for the first time looking towards me. 'My learned Ramappa, Ramappa, never go out after sunset; for there are spirits of all sorts walking in the dark. Especially never once go by the canal after the cows are come home. It is a haunted place, Ramappa.'

'How do you know?' I asked, curious.

'How! With these very eyes, I have seen, Ramappa, I have seen it all. The potter's wife Rangi was unhappy. Poor thing! Poor thing! And one night she had such heavy, heavy sorrow, she ran and jumped into the canal. The other day, when I was coming home in the deadly dark with my little lamb, whom should I see but Rangi—Rangi in a white, broad sari, her hair all floating. She stood in front of me. I shivered and wept. She ran and stood by a tree, yelling in a strange voice! "Away! Away!" I cried. Then suddenly I saw her standing on the bridge, and she jumped into the canal, moaning: "My girl is gone, my child is gone, and I am gone too!" '

My sister trembled. She had a horror of devils. 'Why don't you shut up, you donkey's widow, and not pour out all your Vedantic knowledge?'

'Pardon me, Mother, pardon me,' she begged.

'I have pardoned you again and again, and yet it is the same old story. Always the same *Ramayana*. Why don't you fall into the well like Rangi and turn devil?' My sister was furious.

Javni smiled and hid her face between her knees, timidly. 'How beautiful your brother is!' she murmured after a moment, ecstatic.

'Did I not say he was like a prince! Who knows what incarnation of a god he may be? Who knows?' my sister whispered, patting me, proudly, religiously.

'Sita!' I replied, and touched her lap with tenderness.

'Without Javni I could never have lived in this damned place!' said my sister after a moment's silence.

'And without you, I could not have lived either, Mother!' Her voice was so calm and rich that she seemed to sing.

'In this damned place everything is so difficult,' cursed Sita. '*He* is always struggling with the collections. The villages are few, but placed at great distances from one another. Sometimes he has been away for more than a week, and I should have died of fright had not Javni been with me. And,' she whispered, a little sadly, 'Javni, I am sure, understands my fears, my beliefs. Men, Ramu, can never understand us.'

'Why?' I asked.

'Why? I cannot say. You are too practical and too irreligious. To us everything is mysterious. Our gods are not your gods, your gods not our gods. It is a simple affair.' She seemed sadder still.

'But yet, I have always tried to understand you,' I managed to whisper.

'Of course! of course!' cried my sister, reassured.

'Mother,' muttered Javni, trembling, 'Mother! will you permit me to say one thing?' She seemed to plead.

'Yes!' answered my sister.

'Ramappa, your sister loves you,' said Javni. 'She loves you as though you were her own child. Oh! I wish I had seen her two children! They must have been angels! Perhaps they are in Heaven now—in Heaven! Children go to Heaven! But, Ramappa, what I wanted to say was this. Your sister loves you, talks of you all the time, and says, "If my brother did not live, I should have died long ago".'

'How long have you been with Sita?' I asked Javni, trying to change the subject.

'How long? How long have I been with this family? What do I know? But let me see. The harvest was over and we were husking the grains when they came.'

'How did you happen to find her?' I asked my sister.

'Why, Ramappa,' cried Javni, proud for the first time, 'there is nobody who can work for a Revenue Inspector's family as I. You can go and ask everybody in the town, including every pariah if you like, and they will tell you, "Javni, she is good like a cow," and they will also add that there is no one who can serve a big man like the Revenue Inspector as Javni—as I.' She beat her breast with satisfaction.

'So you are the most faithful servant among the servants here!' I added a little awkwardly.

'Of course!' she cried proudly, her hands folded upon her knees. 'Of course!'

'How many Revenue Inspectors have you served?'

'How many? Now let me see.' Here she counted upon her fingers, one by one, remembering them by how many children they had, what sort of views they had, their caste, their native place, or even how good they had been in giving her two saris, a four-anna tip or a sack of rice.

'Javni,' I said, trying to be a little bit humorous, 'suppose I came here one day, say after ten or fifteen or twenty years, and I am not a Revenue Inspector, and I ask you to serve me. Will you or will you not?'

She looked perplexed, laughed and turned towards my sister for help.

'Answer him!' commanded my sister affectionately.

'But Ramappa,' she cried out, full of happiness, as if she had discovered a solution, 'you cannot but be a big man like our Master, the Revenue Inspector. With your learning and your beauty you cannot be anything else. And, when you come here, of course I will be your servant.'

'But if I am not a Revenue Inspector,' I insisted.

'You must be—you must be!' she cried, as if I were insulting myself.

'All right, I shall be a Revenue Inspector in order to have you,' I joked.

'As if it were not enough that I should bleed myself to death in being one,' added my brother-in-law, as he entered through the back door, dust-covered and breathless.

Javni rose up and ran away as if in holy fear. It was the Master.

'She is a sweet thing,' I said to my sister.

'Almost a mother!' she added, and smiled.

In the byre Javni was talking to the calf.

My brother-in-law was out touring two or three days in the week. On these days Javni usually came to sleep at our house; for my sister had a terror of being alone. And, since it had become a habit, Javni came as usual even when I was there. One evening, I cannot remember why, we had dined early, and unrolling our beds, we lay down when it was hardly sunset. Javni came, peeped from the window and called in a whisper, 'Mother, Mother!'

'Come in, you monkey,' answered my sister.

Javni opened the door and stepped in. She had a sheet in her hand, and, throwing it on the floor, she went straight into the byre where her food was usually kept. I could not bear that. Time and again I had quarrelled with my sister about it all.

But she would not argue with me. 'They are of the lower class, and you cannot ask them to sit and eat with you,' she would say.

'Of course!' I said. 'After all, why not? Are they not like us, like any of us? Only the other day you said you loved her as if she were your elder sister or mother.'

'Yes!' she grunted angrily. 'But affection does not ask you to be irreligious.'

'And what, pray, is being irreligious?' I continued, furious.

'Irreligious. Irreligious. Well, eating with a woman of a lower caste is irreligious. And, Ramu,' she cried desperately, 'I have enough of quarrelling all the time. In the name of our holy mother can't you leave me alone!' There, tears!

'You are inhuman!' I spat, disgusted.

'Go and show your humanity!' she grumbled, and, hiding her face beneath the blanket, she wept harder.

I was really much too ashamed and too angry to stay in my bed. I rose and went into the byre. Javni sat in the dark, swallowing mouthfuls of rice that sounded like a cow chewing the cud. She thought I had come to go into the garden, but I remained beside her, leaning against the wall. She stopped eating and looked deeply embarrassed.

'Javni,' I said tenderly.

'Ramappa!' she answered, confused.

'Why not light a lantern when you eat, Javni?'

'What use?' she replied, and began to chew the cud.

'But you cannot see what you are eating,' I explained.

'I cannot. But there is no necessity to see what you eat.' She laughed as if amused.

'But you must!' I was angry.

'No, Ramappa. I know where my rice is, and I can feel where the pickle is, and that is enough.'

Just at that moment, the cow threw a heapful of dung, which splashed across the cobbled floor.

'Suppose you come with me into the hall,' I cried. I knew I could never convince her.

'No, Ramappa. I am quite well here. I do not want to dirty the floor of the hall.'

'If it is dirty, I will clean it,' I cried, exasperated.

She was silent. In the darkness I saw the shadow of Javni near me, thrown by the faint starlight that came from the garden door. In the corner the cow was breathing hard, and the calf was nibbling at the wisps of hay. It was a terrible moment. The whole misery of the world seemed to be weighing all about and above me. And yet—and yet—the suffering—one seemed to laugh at it all.

'Javni,' I said affectionately, 'do you eat at home like this?'

'Yes, Ramappa.' Her tone was sad.

'And why?'

'The oil is too expensive, Ramappa.'

'But surely you can buy it?' I continued.

'No, Ramappa. It costs an anna a bottle, and it lasts only a week.'

'But an anna is nothing,' I said.

'Nothing! Nothing!' She spoke as if frightened. 'Why, my learned Ramappa, it is what I earn in two days.'

'In two days!' I had rarely been more surprised.

'Yes, Ramappa, I earn one rupee each month.' She seemed content.

I heard an owl hoot somewhere, and far, far away, somewhere too far and too distant for my rude ears to hear, the world wept its silent suffering plaints. Had not the Lord said: 'Whenever there is misery and ignorance, I come'? Oh, when will that day come, and when will the Conch of Knowledge blow?

I had nothing to say. My heart beat fast. And, closing my eyes, I sank into the primal flood, the moving fount of Being. Man, I love you.

Javni sat and ate. The mechanical mastication of the rice seemed to represent her life, her cycle of existence.

'Javni,' I inquired, breaking the silence, 'what do you do with the one rupee?'

'I never take it,' she answered laughing.

'Why don't you take it, Javni?'

'Mother keeps it for me. Now and again she says I work well

and adds an anna or two to my funds, and one day I shall have
enough to buy a sari.'

'And the rest?' I asked.

'The rest? Why, I will buy something for my brother's child.'

'Is your brother poor, Javni?'

'No. But, Ramappa, I love the child.' She smiled.

'Suppose I asked you to give it to me?' I laughed, since I
could not weep.

'Oh, you will never ask me, Ramappa, never. But, Ramappa,
if you should, I would give it to you.' She laughed too, content
and amused.

'You are a wonderful thing!' I murmured.

'At your feet, Ramappa!' She had finished eating, and she
went into the bathroom to wash her hands.

I walked out into the garden and stood looking at the
sparkling heavens. There was companionship in their shining.
The small and the great clustered together in the heart of the
quiet limpid sky. God, knew they caste? Far away a cartman
chanted forth:

> The night is dark;
> Come to me, mother.
> The night is quiet;
> Come to me, friend.

The winds sighed.

On the nights when Javni came to sleep with us, we gossiped
a great deal about village affairs. She had always news to tell us.
One day it would be about the postman Subba's wife, who had
run away with the Mohammedan of the mango shop. On
another day it would be about the miraculous cure of Sata
Venkanna's wife, Kanthi, during her recent pilgrimage to the
Biligiri temple. My sister always took an interest in those things,
and Javni made it her affair to find out everything about everybody. She gossiped the whole evening till we both fell asleep.
My sister usually lay by the window, I near the door, and Javni
at our feet. She slept on a bare wattle-mat, with a cotton sheet

for a cover, and she seemed never to suffer from cold. On one of these nights when we were gossiping, I pleaded with Javni to tell me just a little about her own life. At first she waved aside my idea; but, after a moment when my sister howled at her, she accepted it, still rather unhappily. I was all ears, but my sister was soon snoring comfortably.

Javni was born in the neighbouring village of Kotehalli, where her father cultivated the fields in the winter and washed clothes in the summer. Her mother had always work to do, since there were childbirths almost every day in one village or the other, and, being a hereditary midwife, she was always sent for. Javni had four sisters and two brothers, of whom only her brother Bhima remained. She loved her parents, and they loved her too; and, when she was eighteen, she was duly married to a boy whom they had chosen from Malkad. The boy was good and affectionate, and he never once beat her. He too was a washerman, and 'What do you think?' said Javni proudly, 'he washed clothes for the Maharaja, when he came here.'

'Really!' I exclaimed.

And she continued. Her husband was, as I have said, a good man, and he really cared for her. He never made her work too much, and he always cooked for her when she fell sick. One day, however, as the gods decided it, a snake bit him while he was washing clothes by the river, and, in spite of all the magic that the barber Subba applied, he died that very evening, crying to the last, 'Javni, Javni, my Javni.' (I should have expected her to weep here. But she continued without any exclamations or sighs.) Then came all the misfortunes one after the other, and yet she knew they were nothing, for, above all, she said, Goddess Talakamma moved and reigned.

Her husband belonged to a family of three brothers and two sisters. The elder brother was a wicked fellow, who played cards and got drunk two days out of three. The second was her husband, and the third was a haughty young fellow, who had already, it was known, made friends with the concubine Siddi, the former mistress of the priest Rangappa. He treated his wife as if she were an ox and once he actually beat her till she was

bleeding and unconscious. There were many children in the
family, and since one of the sisters-in-law also lived in the same
village, her children too came to play in the house. So Javni
lived on happily, working at home as usual and doing her little
to earn for the family funds.

She never knew, she said, how it all happened, but one day a
policeman came, frightened everybody, and took away her
elder brother-in-law for some reason that nobody understood.
The women were all terrified and everybody wept. The people
in the town began to spit at them as they passed by, and left
cattle to graze away all the crops in the fields to show their
hatred and their revenge. Shame, poverty and quarrels, these
followed one another. And because the elder brother-in-law was
in prison and the younger with his mistress, the women at home
made her life miserable. ' "You dirty widow!" they would say
and spit on me. I wept and sobbed and often wanted to go and
fall into the river. But I knew Goddess Talakamma would be
angry with me, and I stopped each time I wanted to kill myself.
One day, however, my elder sister-in-law became so evil-
mouthed that I ran away from the house. I did not know to
whom to go, since I knew nobody and my brother hated me—
he always hated me. But anyway, Ramappa,' she said, 'anyway,
a sister is a sister. You cannot deny that the same mother has
suckled you both.'

'Of course not!' I said.

'But he never treated me as you treat your sister.'

'So, you are jealous, you ill-boding widow!' swore my sister,
waking up. She always thought people hated or envied her.

'No, Mother, no,' Javni pleaded.

'Go on!' I said.

'I went to my brother,' she continued. 'As soon as his wife
saw me she swore and spat and took away her child that was
playing on the verandah, saying it would be bewitched. After
a moment my brother came out.

' "Why have you come?" he asked me.

' "I am without a home," I said.

' "You dirty widow, how can you find a house to live in,

when you carry misfortune wherever you set your foot?"

'I simply wept.

' "Weep, weep!" he cried, "weep till your tears flood the Cauvery. But you will not get a morsel of rice from me. No, not a morsel!"

' "No," I said. "I do not want a morsel of rice. I want only a palm-width of shelter to put myself under."

'He seemed less angry. He looked this side and that and roared: "Do you promise me never to quarrel with anyone?"

' "Yes!" I answered, still weeping.

' "Then, for the peace of the spirit of my father, I will give you the little hut by the garden door. You can sit, weep, eat, shit, die—do what you like there," he said. I trembled. In the meantime my sister-in-law came back. She frowned and thumped the floor, swearing at me and calling me a prostitute, a donkey, a witch. Ramappa, I never saw a woman like that. She makes my life a life of tears.'

'How?' I asked.

'How! I cannot say. It is ten years or twenty since I set foot in their house. And every day I wake up with "donkey's wife" or "prostitute" in my ears.'

'But you don't have anything to do with her?' I said.

'I don't. But the child sometimes comes to me because I love it and then my sister-in-law rushes out, roaring like a tigress, and says she will flay me to death if I touch the child again.'

'You should not touch it,' I said.

'Of course I would not if I had my own child. But, Ramappa, that little boy loves me.'

'And why don't they want you to touch him?'

'Because they say I am a witch and an evil spirit.' She wept.

'Who says it?'

'They. Both of them say it. But still, Ramappa'—here she suddenly turned gay—'I always keep mangoes and cakes that Mother gives me and save them all for the little boy. So he runs away from his mother each time the door is open. He is such a sweet, sweet thing.' She was happy.

'How old is he?' I asked.

'Four.'

'Is he their only child?'

'No. They have four more—all grown up. One is already a boy as big as you.'

'And the others, do they love you?'

'No. They all hate me, they all hate me—except that child.'

'Why don't you adopt a child?'

'No, Ramappa. I have a lamb, and that is enough.'

'You have a lamb too!' I said, surprised.

'Yes, a lamb for the child to play with now, and, when the next Durga festival comes, I will offer it to Goddess Talakamma.'

'Offer it to the Goddess! Why, Javni? Why not let it live?'

'Don't speak sacrilege, Ramappa. I owe a lamb every three years to the Goddess.'

'And what does she give in return?'

'What do you say! What!' She was angry. 'All! Everything! Should I live if that Goddess did not protect me? Would that child come to me if the Goddess did not help me? Would Mother be so good to me if the Goddess did not bless me? Why, Ramappa, everything is hers. O Great Goddess Talakamma, give everybody good health and long life and all progeny! Protect me, Mother!' She was praying.

'What will she give me if I offer a lamb?' I asked.

'Everything, Ramappa. You will grow learned; you will become a big man; you will marry a rich wife. Ramappa,' she said, growing affectionate all of a sudden, 'I have already been praying for you. When Mother said she had a brother, I said to the Goddess, "Goddess, keep that boy strong and virtuous and give him all the eight riches of Heaven and earth." '

'Do you love me more or less than your brother's child?' I asked, to change the subject.

She was silent for a moment.

'You don't know?' I said.

'No, Ramappa. I have been thinking. I offer the lamb to the Goddess for the sake of the child. I have not offered a lamb for you. So how can I say whom I love more?'

'The child!' I said.

'No, no, I love you as much, Ramappa.'

'Will you adopt me?' No, I was not joking.

She broke into fits of laughter which woke up my sister.

'Oh, shut up!' cried Sita.

'Do you know Javni is going to adopt me?'

'Adopt you! Why does she not go and fall into the river?' she roared, and went to sleep again.

'If you adopt me, Javni, I will work for you and give you food to eat.'

'No, learned Ramappa. A Brahmin is not meant to work. You are the "chosen ones".'

Chosen ones, indeed! 'No, we are not!' I murmured.

'You are. You are. The sacred books are yours. The Vedas are yours. You are all, you are all, you are the twice-born. We are your servants, Ramappa—your slaves.'

'I am not a Brahmin,' I said half-jokingly, half-seriously.

'You are. You are. You want to make fun of me.'

'No, Javni, suppose you adopt me?'

She laughed again.

'If you do not adopt me, I shall die now and grow into a lamb in my next life and you will buy it. What will you do then?'

She did not say anything. It was too perplexing.

'Now,' I said, feeling sleepy, 'now, Javni, go to sleep and think again tomorrow morning whether you will adopt me or not.'

'Adopt you! You are a god, Ramappa, a god! I cannot adopt you.'

I dozed away. Only in the stillness I heard Javni saying: 'Goddess, Great Goddess, as I vowed, I will offer thee my lamb. Protect the child, protect Mother, protect her brother, protect Master, O Goddess! Protect me!'

The Goddess stood silent, in the little temple by the Cauvery, amidst the whisper of the woods.

A July morning, two summers later. Our cart rumbled over the boulders of the street, and we were soon at the village

square. Javni was running behind the cart, with tears rolling
down her cheeks. For one full week I had seen her weeping all
the time, all the time dreading the day when we should leave
her and she would see us no more. She was breathless. But she
walked fast, keeping pace with the bullocks. I was with my sister
in the back of the cart, and my brother-in-law sat in front,
beside the cartman. My sister too was sad. In her heart she
knew she was leaving a friend. Yes, Javni had been her friend,
her only friend. Now and again they gazed at each other, and
I could see Javni suddenly sobbing like a child.

'Mother, Mother,' she would say approaching the cart, 'don't
forget me.'

'I will not. No, I assure you, I will not.'

Now my sister too was in tears.

'Even if she should, I will not,' I added. I myself should have
wept had I not been so civilized.

When we touched the river, it was already broad morning.
Now, in the summer, there was so little water that the ferry was
not plying and we were going to wade through. The cartman
said he would rest the bullocks for a moment, and I got out
partly to breathe the fresh air and more to speak to Javni.

'Don't weep,' I said to her.

'Ramappa, how can I help but weep? Shall I ever see again
a family of gods like yours? Mother was kind to me, kind like a
veritable goddess. You were so, so good to me, and Master—.'
Here she broke again into sobs.

'No, Javni. In contact with a heart like yours, who will not
bloom into a god?'

But she simply wept. My words meant nothing to her. She
was nervous, and she trembled over and over again. 'Mother,
Mother,' she would say between her sobs, 'O Mother!'

The cartman asked me to get in. I got into the cart with a
heavy heart. I was leaving a most wonderful soul. I was in. The
cartman cried, 'Hoy, hoyee!' And the bulls stepped into the
river.

Till we were on the other bank, I could see Javni sitting on a
rock, and looking towards us. In my heart I seemed still to hear

her sobs. A huge pipal rose behind her, and, across the blue waters of the river and the vast, vast sky above her, she seemed so small, just a spot in space, recedingly real. Who was she?

From *The Cow of the Barricades
and Other Stories*, 1947

MANOHAR MALGONKAR

Manohar Malgonkar was born in Bombay in 1913 and was educated at Karnatak College, Dharwar and Bombay University. Between 1942 and 1952 he served in the Maratha Light Infantry and rose to the rank of Lieutenant-Colonel. After a spell as a big-game hunter, he settled down in Jagalbet near Belgaum where he now runs a farm. Essentially a story-teller, Malgonkar writes: 'I do strive to write the sort of novel I also like to read, full of meat, exciting, well-constructed, plausible and with a lot of action—in short, to tell a good story.' His works include *Distant Drum* (1960), *Combat of Shadows* (1962), *The Princes* (1963), *A Bend in the Ganges* (1964), *The Devil's Wind: Nana Saheb's Story* (1972) and *Spy in Amber* (1971), a screenplay.

Malgonkar's experience of action in the Second World War has offered him extensive material for several of his short stories. 'Bachcha Lieutenant' is one of his most interesting tales of military adventure, packed with drama and suspense. It is a story of loyalty and commitment to duty which transcend all barriers of nationality. If Jamadar Tukaram Shindey exposes himself to grave risk in collecting secret information about the enemy's movements, his British officer, Lieutenant Wilson, sets out at great personal risk in search of his 'missing' scout. As Wilson approaches the heavily mined Japanese track, Tukaram shouts out his warning only to find himself ambushed by the enemy and riddled with bullets. To rescue his scout, the British officer keeps pressing forward under a hail of fire, till both of them slump on the ground, dead.

The story moves relentlessly on to a dramatic climax, and the style, rigorously terse and vividly descriptive, seems to be most appropriate to the central action.

Bachcha Lieutenant

The dog barked, alarmed and frightened, the yelping, whining, trailing-off-into-a-howl sort of bark of a piedog, and Jamadar Tukaram Shindey froze in his tracks, fighting the impulse to fling himself on the ground. He could hear his own quick gasping breathing and feel his heart pounding violently against his chest, and in his head surged all the thoughts, confused and fragmentary, that come to one in the face of imminent death—when one expects an instantaneous hail of enemy bullets.

But with equal suddenness, he realized that he was being foolish, nervous like a new rangroot, and not the veteran soldier he was on his second campaign in Burma. There was no danger of death. The night was pitch dark, you couldn't see your hand in front of your face. So long as you kept your head, so long as you did not make any noise that would give away your position, you were all right.

Someone gave an order. The dog stopped barking, abruptly, and the Arakan jungle resumed its heavy silence. Cautiously, inch by inch, Jamadar Tukaram Shindey lowered himself down, and lay prone on the warm earth. His clothes were wet with sweat.

He unbuckled his belt, and took out from the haversack a thick roll of dry chapatis and two large onions. He peeled off two onions and began to munch his dinner, biting off the chapatis and the onions alternately.

Two hundred yards away, where the cart track dipped into the dry bed of the Chaung, the dog scratched his ear, and curled up and lay shivering in spite of the stuffy, oppressive heat. He was a stringy, mustard and white mongrel, and he was kept permanently hungry so that he should always remain wide awake. Three days ago, he had been taken from his village near Bhutidaung, and now he was tied to a post near the bend of the road with strong coir rope. He felt angry and vicious and ready to snap at all times. He was an unwilling and bewildered participant in the war, but he made an alert sentry.

To Jamadar Tukaram, the dog barking like that in the middle of the jungle at least a mile away from the nearest hamlet, could only mean one thing; there was a Japanese position near the bend of the road.

Tukaram looked longingly at the two remaining chapatis. Then, folding them carefully so that they shouldn't break into pieces, he put them back in the mess tin. After that he unslung his water bottle and put it to his mouth.

The night was warm, the forest giving out a steamy heat, and there wasn't a breath of air. Tukaram took a tiny sip to wet his tongue and the water was cloying and tepid, as though the heat had made it thicker, and it tasted foully of chlorine. He was thirsty and wanted to go on drinking, allowing the water to run extravagantly gurgling down his throat. But after three unsatisfying gulps he stopped. This self-discipline too had become a matter of habit. While on patrol, however close you were to camp, three mouthfuls was all that you allowed yourself with a meal.

Actually, Jamadar Tukaram could have gone back to the company position and had as much water to drink as he wanted. And perhaps the Intelligence Officer, Lieutenant Wilson, would have even offered him some tea. The I.O. always seemed to be drinking tea.

Yes, Tukaram could have gone back to his unit, for his mission had been accomplished. He and another scout had been sent out to find how far down the Taungdaw road the first enemy position was, and as usual, Jamadar Tukaram had left the other scout behind.

He always preferred to go on a patrol of this sort alone. He was a jungle man, born and brought up in the jungles of North Kanara, and he used to be a big-game tracker before he joined the army. To him, there was nothing strange about the Burmese jungles. He could move in them as silently as any animal of the jungle itself, and as long as he was sent out on his own, he could get all the information they wanted. But taking someone else along was always dangerous. It certainly complicated matters.

That had been the. cause of his first clash with Lieutenant Wilson. The new I.O., Wilson, a bespectacled, fair-haired, thin young man with a large adam's apple, had joined the 4th Satpuras barely two months ago. He was nineteen years old, and he had not seen any action so far. He read poetry, and he didn't drink or smoke or use swearwords, and he was serious at all times. As such, he was unlike any officer the 4th Satpuras had had so far, and God knows they had had a goodly number of queer ones since the war started. Everyone called him the *Bachcha* Lieutenant.

But Wilson had done an Intelligence Course at the School in Karachi, and had managed to get a D grading at the course, and he was convinced that he knew all about how patrols should be carried out.

'No use going out on your own, Jamadar saab,' he had said, pronouncing the 'saab' as though it rhymed with 'nab'. 'Two can observe much better than one.'

'Two people moving about in the jungle make much more noise than one, sir,' Tukaram had pointed out.

'Well, supposing you went on patrol by yourself, Jamadar saab, and you were shot down or captured. Who would bring back the information?'

'There is much more likelihood of both of us being killed or captured, sir, if two of us were to go, than there is of my being killed or captured if I went by myself,' Tukaram had said.

But it had been no use. The Bachcha Lieutenant had ordered that his intelligence personnel must never go out on patrol except in batches of at least two. Actually, he himself preferred a patrol of four, particularly at night. But in view of the shortage of men, he could not always insist on patrols of four.

So, soon after sunset, Jamadar Tukaram Shindey and Haval-dar Ranga had set out along the Taungdaw cart track, but after they had gone about a mile, Tukaram had left the other scout behind, telling him to wait until he returned. And now he was all alone, lying on his back, trying to fight a desperate longing for a cigarette, and hardly a couple of hundred yards away from an enemy position.

For a whole hour, Tukaram had waited in the hope of being able to find out something more about the enemy. If they only talked or coughed or made some noise, he would have a rough idea of how many there were. But there had been no tell-tale sounds. After the barking of the dog, and the sharp word of command, everything had been silent.

Tukaram Shindey shook his head and cursed silently. Then he put on his equipment and without making the slightest noise, slid away from his position and made his way back to the track junction where he had left the other scout.

Two low whistles repeated at two-second intervals brought Havaldar Ranga out of the shadows. The first thing that Tukaram said to him was, 'Do you think you can find your way back to camp?'

'Why aren't you coming back?'

'I have discovered a Jap position, but unless I watch them in daylight I can't find out anything more about them. I propose to go back and·take a position near them and see what they are up to, find out how many there are, what weapons they possess, and things like that.'

'Of course, I can find my way back; it is hardly a mile away to camp. But Bachcha saab is not going to like your going on your own like this.'

'I'm sure he won't. But that can't be helped.'

'He is bound to blow me up. What shall I tell him?'

'Tell him I ordered you to go back.'

'Yes, sir,' said Havaldar Ranga.

Then Tukaram gave the other all the information he had obtained. It wasn't much. There was an enemy position approximately one and a half miles down the Taungdaw track. Strength not known, weapons not known. He gave a four-figure map reference. He told Ranga to say that Jamadar Tukaram was going to try and keep the enemy under observation during the next day, to be able to make ‘a fuller report in the evening.

'Is that all?' asked Ranga.

'That's all. I say, you haven't got any haversack rations you can spare, have you? I will have to carry on the whole of tomorrow on two dry chapatis and my last onion.'

'No, I have finished all mine,' said Ranga. 'I always feel very hungry when I am on patrol.'

'Oh, never mind. You are sure you can make your way back?'

'Of course, I can find my way back,' the other had said, sounding hurt, and within twenty minutes after that was hopelessly lost. He never returned to the battalion. Early the next morning as he was still wandering in a daze along a footpath in the forest, he had been neatly picked out by a Japanese sniper.

As soon as Jamadar Tukaram Shindey was back at the spot where he had eaten his dinner, he put his head on his haversack and fell asleep. He woke up before dawn, and for a long time lay straining to locate any sounds coming from the direction of the track. Just before first light, he drank another three mouthfuls of water and ate one of the chapatis. After that, he began to crawl forward towards where he had heard the dog bark the previous night.

He moved through the undergrowth silently, crouching and crawling on his stomach and every now and then raising his head to see how far he was from the track.

A large uprooted tree lay between him and the open track, and if he could only get behind the tree, he could keep a longish stretch of the road under observation. The only snag in getting behind the fallen tree would be that it would then be impossible to get away from there without being seen. In the grey-green darkness of the jungle dawn it was easy enough to approach the tree unseen, but once there it was almost certain that he would have to wait until evening to get away.

But it was equally apparent that if he wanted to keep the track under observation, the tree was the best place, and cautiously, his stomach feeling empty with nervousness, he made his way through the open ground to the tree.

He could now observe the Taungdaw cart track for a stretch

of nearly 200 yards, with the bend of the track directly below him, hardly fifty yards away.

He was just in time. As soon as the first light of the summer sun touched the tops of the trees, the Japanese soldiers began to come out one by one, and soon, there were almost twenty of them on the road. Jamadar Tukaram's unshaven face contorted itself into a fearsome grin. With a bren, he could have picked them all out; at times they were bunched up beautifully, making an ideal target. One burst, and half of them would lie dead. But there was no point in thinking about a bren—he didn't have a bren with him. All he had was a sten, with three spare magazines, and six 63 grenades fitted with four-second fuses.

But it was much more important to observe these men and take back the information to the I.O. than to kill a few of them. Because once you had observed them well, you could come with the necessary number of men and finish them off in one go.

The Japanese soldiers were digging shallow trenches right in the middle of the track. Tukaram wondered what they were up to. Surely, they were not digging slit trenches in the middle of the open track.

But their purpose was soon apparent. They were obviously putting down AP mines and laying boobytrap wires along the track. Fascinated, Tukaram watched the little khaki figures working with the jerky movements of mechanical toys. In no time at all, they had put in half a dozen brass AP mines and laid several strands of trip wire across the track. Then they had put back the earth and the leaves on the road to make the surface look undisturbed.

They finished off soon after nine and then posting a sentry on either side of the bend they began to dig their foxholes on the opposite slope of the hill. Methodically, putting their heads close to the ground, they cleared the intervening undergrowth to give their guns an unrestricted field of fire. Their purpose was clear. They would sit in their foxholes, guarding the track, and ambush any enemy troops that happened to be walking along the track.

Jamadar Tukaram congratulated himself on having come back for a second look. If he had waited until daylight, he would never have been able to approach so close to their position.

The craving for a cigarette had come back, stronger than ever, and in an effort to drag his mind away, Tukaram began to think about his impending interrogation by the I.O. He was quite looking forward to it although he knew that the Bachcha Lieutenant would be peeved with him for disregarding his orders, and that he would try to be aloof and frosty and take down the vital information brought back by Tukaram as though he were writing up the log for a 'blank' patrol.

Tukaram pictured himself telling the I.O. all the details: nearest enemy position—one and a half miles along the Taung-daw track, at map reference, this, this, this, this, this, this; strength—approximately thirty. And then he could almost hear Wilson asking in that squeaky voice of his: 'How approximately, saab?' Wilson always suspected approximate figures. 'Well, not more than thirty-two and not less than twenty-eight, sir,' he would say. 'They are dug in about thirty yards up the slope of the hill to the north of the track and they are armed with rifles, two LMGs and a Japanese type mortar, and of course, the dog . . . the damned dog. . . .'

It was nearly midday and all of a sudden, the dog who had been lying quietly in the sun tied up to a stake buried in the middle of the track, began to yelp, and Tukaram saw a thickset Japanese soldier clumsily swiping at the dog with a heavy spade. He missed twice, and for that time, the dog continued his furious yelping and then, as the next blow hit him squarely on the skull, fell limply on the ground and lay silently twitching for some seconds before he became absolutely still.

There was a clammy, choking feeling in Tukaram's throat. 'You dog-killing . . . ,' he said to himself, 'you s. . . .'

The Japanese soldier had dragged away the dog's body and was shovelling earth on the road in order to obliterate the bloodstains and Tukaram had a wild desire to let him have a burst from his sten. Instead, he decided to have a drink of water.

It took a long time for him to unbuckle the water bottle and then he brought it slowly to his mouth and with deliberate recklessness drained all its contents, knowing that he had nothing to wash down his last chapati and onion which he had been saving up. The sight of the dog, the faithful sentry of the previous night, being finished off in that brutal manner was somehow more horrifying than many things he had seen in this war.

But as a soldier, he could see the reason why the dog had been killed. He was a two-edged weapon. He would act as a sentry, of course, but he could just as easily give your own position away by barking, and if you wanted to lie waiting for an ambush, it was no use having a dog around. Soon, all was quiet again, and the thin red meandering line of the cart track looked desolate and deserted. Even the sentries had been withdrawn.

Jamadar Tukaram grinned, and smacked his lips. At least he knew exactly where they had dug their position. Tomorrow he would himself lead a party and finish them off neatly, as they sat in their trenches with their LMGs trained on the bend of the road, 'The dog-killing swines!'

But as far as Jamadar Tukaram was concerned, tomorrow never came. Angrily, biting his nails nervously, Lieutenant Wilson had waited from early morning for the return of his two scouts. As the day wore on, he had become more and more fidgety and irritable. He had not heard any firing during the night and refused to believe that both his scouts had been killed. It was imperative to find out exactly how far the nearest enemy position was, and that cocky Jamadar of his had let him down. Both he and the other scout sent out the previous evening had failed to return.

At midday, Wilson sent for his Subedar. 'I want two jawans,' he told him. 'They are to take haversack rations, torches, stens with three spare magazines, and six grenades each. Rubber-soled shoes.' Lieutenant Wilson was nothing if not thorough. 'I am going on a patrol myself down the Taungdaw road. You will have to act for me,' he added.

Tapping his rubbersoled shoes with his fingers to keep his feet from going to sleep, Jamadar Tukaram Shindey squirmed behind the fallen tree. Despite the cramp and his hunger, he was pleased with himself, and waited patiently for the release from his position that darkness would bring.

But he did not have to wait for darkness. Late in the afternoon he saw from his vantage point three men in olive green uniforms walking along the cart tracks from the direction of the Satpura position. He watched them in disbelief, coming nearer and nearer to the death-trap in the bend of the track, walking carefully, watching both sides of the track and keeping dispersed. He could see Lieutenant Wilson's thin, ungainly figure in the lead followed by two other men who were still too far away to be identified. 'Blast that Bachcha of a Lieutenant Wilson,' he said to himself. 'Blast him.' And then he acted.

'Stop, sahib! Halt!' he shouted at the top of his voice. 'Ambush, ambush, stop,' and then he charged at the trenches of the enemy, firing his stengun and yelling hoarsely at the same time.

Close to where the dog had been killed was an anthill beside the road, and Tukaram flung himself behind it and began to hurl his grenades: one, two, three; they went off with resounding booms amidst the din and whine of enemy bullets. As he was about to pull out the pin from another grenade he felt a white-hot pain in his shoulder and fell down with an oath, the grenade dropping from his suddenly powerless hands.

Lieutenant Wilson and his two guides had flung themselves face downwards on the road and the bullets spattered the ground in front of them on the bend. From there, they watched Jamadar Tukaram's single-handed attack against the Japanese position. They saw him fall down and then rise, shouting at them, 'Get back, you fools, get back, you fool Bachcha Lieutenant! There are thirty Japs dug in there!' They saw his shirt redden with the blood squirting from his shoulder and saw him pull out the pin from the grenade with his teeth and fling it at the enemy trenches with his left hand, shouting, 'Take that, you dog-killing . . .' and then fall down again.

And then the Bachcha Lieutenant had risen to his feet uttering an unaccustomed oath and running madly into the dust rising from the bullets which kicked the road near the anthill. With open mouths, his two scouts watched him run through the screen of dust and reach the anthill unharmed. They saw him pick up Jamadar Tukaram Shindey, and they were even more aghast when they heard the Jamadar shouting at the sahib in a voice that could be heard distinctly above the storm of bullets, 'Get back, sahib, get back, you fool Bachcha, run into the jungle!' They saw the Bachcha Lieutenant pick up the Jamadar and sling him across his shoulder and run and stumble and fall, and rise heavily and run again. And they saw him stumble and fall again and lie in a heap in the bend of the cart track in the bed of the Chaung. And they saw more and more bullets riddling the two prone bodies making their limbs twitch with each hit.

The rest of Lieutenant Wilson's patrol got back to the battalion. Neither Jamadar Tukaram Shindey nor the Bachcha Lieutenant ever knew just how much they had contributed to each other's death.

From Bombay Beware, 1975

KHWAJA AHMAD ABBAS

A versatile writer, Khwaja Ahmad Abbas is a novelist, short-story writer, historian, biographer, journalist, screenwriter, film producer and director. Born in Panipat in 1914, he took his degree in law from Aligarh Muslim University in 1935 and joined *The Bombay Chronicle* as reporter and sub-editor. From 1939 to 1947, he edited the Sunday edition of the paper, and since then has been a regular columnist for *Blitz*. His published works are too numerous to mention, but his best-known fictional works are *Tomorrow Is Ours!* (1943), *Rice and Other Stories* (1947), *Inqilab* (1955), *Black Sun and Other Stories* (1963), *When Night Falls* (1968), *Mera Nam Joker* (1970), *Maria* (1971) and *The Walls of Glass* (1975). His most recent work of importance is an autobiography *I Am Not an Island* (1976)—a book which clearly demonstrates his deep personal commitment to society.

The very first story by Abbas, '*Ababeel*' ('Sparrows'), was originally written in Urdu and published in *Jamia* in 1937. It was later translated by the author into English and published in *Indian Literature* (London) the following year. Rahim Khan, a small farmer, is forced to abandon his choice of a career and wife in deference to his parents' wishes to marry a woman of their choice, and follow his traditional calling. Embittered, he takes out his frustration by beating his bullocks, bullying the villagers and tyrannizing his wife and children. Left alone in his middle years, he develops a strange kinship with sparrows that have lodged in his thatched roof, and he gives his life to save the birds' nest from a monsoon downpour. The story is, despite the hate that threads through it, a moving study of the human need to love.

Sparrows

The sun was setting behind the mango grove which fringed the western extremity of the village when Rahim Khan returned from the fields. Broad and strong despite his fifty odd years, with the plough on his shoulders, and driving his two oxen, he walked through the main street of the village with a haughty and un-friendly air. As he approached the chaupal where a dozen or so peasants were collected for their evening smoke, the hilarious tones of gossip died down to cautious whispers. It was only when he had vanished round the corner and the heavy tread of his footsteps was heard no more that Kallu, passing the com-munal hookah to another, remarked: 'There goes the hard-hearted devil!' To which Nanha, the fat sweet-seller, added, 'He is getting worse and worse every day. Only yesterday he beat poor Ramoo's child for throwing a pebble at his oxen.' Ram-nath, the officious Zaildar, volunteered further details of Rahim Khan's recent cruelties. 'And the other day he very nearly killed my mare for straying into his field.' The Zaildar, of course, thought it quite irrelevant to mention that the straying of his mare had been specially planned by his own mischievous sons. The old grey-haired patel was, as usual, the last to open his toothless mouth. And as usual, his words were prefaced by a pious invocation to the Almighty. 'Hari Ram! Hari Ram!' he muttered, 'I have never seen such a cruel man. He has com-passion neither for the child nor for the helpless animal. No wonder his own sons have run away from home.'

The subject of their conversation, meanwhile, had reached his hut which, almost symbolically, stood gaunt and aloof, at a distance from the neighbouring cluster of houses. Leaning the plough up against the low wall of his house, he proceeded to tie the oxen to a pair of big wooden stakes embedded in the ground just in front of the doorway.

'Bhai Rahim Khan!' an obsequious voice said behind him as he was about to enter the house.

'What is it?' he gruffly queried turning round to address the old woman who had come out of the house nearest his own. As she hesitated to speak he fired a volley of questions: 'What is it? I won't eat you. Why don't you speak, woman? Has your son been arrested again for revenue arrears or has your daughter-in-law delivered another baby?'

As he stopped for breath, the woman summoned up all her courage to utter two words 'Your wife. . . .'

'. . . has run away,' he completed the sentence with a grin which broadened with the realization that he had guessed right.

'No, no,' the woman hastily explained with an apologetic look, as if she herself were responsible for his wife's absence, 'She has only gone to her brother at Nurpur and will be back in a few days.'

'Bah!' he flung back at her, opening the door. He knew that his wife would never come back.

Seething with inward wrath he entered the dark hut and sat down on the charpoy. A cat mewed in a corner. Finding no one else on whom to vent his anger he flung it out, slamming the door with violence.

There was no one to give him water to wash his dust-laden feet and hands, no one to give him supper, no one whom he could curse and beat. Rahim Khan felt uncomfortable and unhappy. He had always been angry with his wife when she was there, but her absence angered him still more.

'So she's gone,' he mused, lying down on the cot, having decided to go to sleep without his food. During the thirty years of their married life he had always felt that she would leave him one day and, at one time, he had even hoped she would. Six years ago, his eldest son Bundu had run away from home because of a more than usually severe beating. Three years later, the younger one Nuru joined his brother. Since that day, Rahim Khan felt sure his wife, too, would run away to her brother's house. But now that she had gone, he felt unhappy—not sorry, no, for he had never loved his wife—but only uncomfortable as if a necessary piece of furniture had been removed. With her

gone, on whom could he shower the outpourings of an embittered heart?

For thirty years his wife had been both the symbol and target
of all his grievances against family, against society, against life.

As a youth there had been none in the village to beat him
in feats of athletic skill—in wrestling, in kabadi, in diving from
the canal bridge. He had loved a girl, and had wanted to join
a touring circus which happened to pass through the village.
In the circus, he had felt, lay the key to his ambitions—a career
after his own heart—travel—fame. And in Radha, the daughter
of Ram Charan, the village banya, he thought he had found
his soul-mate. He had first noticed her watching him at a
wrestling match and it had been the greatest moment of his
life when, standing up after vanquishing his adversary, he had
found Radha looking at him with the light of love in her eyes.
After that there had been a few brief and furtive meetings when
the unlettered but romantic youth had declared his love in
passionate though halting words. But his parents had killed
both ambitions. Circus work was too lowly and immoral for a
respectable peasant. Anyway, his father, grandfather and all
his ancestors had tilled the land, so he too had to do it. As for
marrying Radha, a Hindu, a Kafir, the very idea was infamous,
and irreligious.

For some time, Rahim Khan, with youthful resentment, toyed
with the idea of open rebellion. But the tradition of centuries of
serfdom ran in his blood and however indignant he might have
felt at his father's severity, he could not summon enough courage
to defy paternal authority and social traditions. After a few
days, the circus left the village without Rahim Khan, and the
furtive romance with Radha, too, came to an abrupt end.
Rahim Khan's father slyly suggested to Ram Charan that his
daughter was now fifteen and ought to have been married long
ago, not failing to hint at the disastrous consequences of late
marriages. Within a few weeks Radha was married to Ram Lal,
a middle-aged, pot-bellied banya of the neighbouring village.
With a few sad tears shed in the solitude of the night in memory
of her hopeless romance with Rahim Khan, she quickly re-

conciled herself to her fate and proceeded forthwith to be the mother of half-a-dozen children.

Rahim Khan also married. He had, of course, no choice in the matter. His parents selected the girl, fixed the date, ordered some gaudy clothes for him and some silver ornaments for his bride, sat him on a horse and, to the beat of a brass band, took him to the girl's house where the Nikah was duly performed. To the Kazi's formal questions Rahim Khan mechanically nodded his head. Any other course was impossible. Nobody, of course, cared to ask the shy little girl who sat huddled in a dark room only dimly conscious of the fate to which she had been condemned. After the ceremony, Rahim Khan's father, in a mood of self-congratulation, boasted to his wife: 'See how meekly he obeyed me. You always feared he might refuse to fall in with our arrangements. I know these youngsters. They are apt to be restless if their marriage is delayed. That is why our fathers believed in marrying away their children early. Now he will be all right.'

At that very moment, standing on the threshold of the room where his wife awaited him much as a sheep awaits the butcher, Rahim Khan made a terrible resolve to avenge himself on his parents, his family, on society. He held them all responsible for the frustration of his life's dreams. And in his confused, illogical mind he regarded his bride as the symbol of the persecution to which he had been subjected. On her he would wreak his vengeance. Iron entered his hitherto kindly soul as he rudely pushed open the door.

That was thirty years ago, Rahim Khan reflected as he lay there on his cot in the dark hut. And hadn't he had his revenge? For thirty years he had ill-treated his wife, his children and his bullocks, quarrelled with everyone in the village and made himself the most hated person in the whole community. The thought of being so universally detested gave him grim satisfaction.

No one in the village, of course, understood or tried to understand the reasons for this strange transformation of the cheerful and kind young man into the beast that he had become. At first their attitude towards him was one of astonished hostility, but later it changed to indifference mingled with fear. Of understanding and sympathy he received none. Shunned by everyone, with a bitterness ever gnawing at his heart, Rahim Khan sought consolation in the unquestioned authority over his wife which society allowed him.

For thirty years his wife had submitted to his persecution with the slave-like docility that is the badge of her tribe. Lately, indeed, she had become so used to corporal chastisement that it seemed unnatural if a whole week passed without a beating. To Rahim Khan beating his wife had become a part of his very existence. As sleep gathered round him, his last thought was whether he would be able to endure a life without having an opportunity to indulge in what had now become his second nature. It was perhaps the only moment when Rahim Khan had a feeling, not exactly of affection, for his wife, but of loneliness without her. Never before had he realized how much the woman he hated was a part of his life.

When he awoke it was already late forenoon and he started the day by cursing his wife, for it was she who used to wake him early every morning. But he was in no great hurry today. Lazily he got up and after his ablutions, milked the goats for his breakfast which consisted of the remains of the previous day's chapatis soaked in the fresh milk. Then he sat down for a smoke, with his beloved hookah beside him. Now the hut was warm and alight with the rays of the sun streaming in through the open window. In a corner they revealed some cobwebs and, having already decided to absent himself from his fields, he thought he would tidy his hut. Tying some rags to the end of the long pole, he was about to remove the cobwebs when he saw a nest in the thatched roof. Two sparrows were fluttering in and out, twittering constantly.

His first impulse was to wreck the nest with one stroke of his pole but something within him made him desist. Throwing down the pole, he brought a stool and climbed up on it to get a better view of the sparrows' home. Two little featherless mites of red flesh, baby sparrows hardly a day old, lay inside, while their parents hovered round Rahim Khan's face, twittering threateningly. He barely had a glimpse of the inside of the nest when the mother sparrow attacked him.

'Oh damn, you vixen, you might have plucked out my eye,' exclaimed Rahim Khan with his characteristic hollow laugh and climbed down from his perch. He was strangely amused by the little bird's heroic efforts to save their home and children. The sparrow's nest suffered no harm that day and peace reigned in Rahim Khan's hut.

Next day he resumed his daily work. Still, no one talked to him in the village. From morning till late in the afternoon he would toil in the field, ploughing the furrow and watering the crops but he returned home before sunset. Then he would lie on his cot, smoking his hookah and watching with lively interest the antics of the sparrow family. The two little ones had now grown into fine young birds and he called them Nuru and Bundu after his lost sons whom he had not seen for several years. The four sparrows were his only friends in the world. His neighbours were still frightened of him and regarded his recent peaceful behaviour with suspicion. They were genuinely astonished that for some time no one had seen him beating his bullocks. Nathoo and Chhiddoo themselves were happy and grateful and their bruised bodies had almost healed.

One monsoon evening, when the sky was overcast with threatening clouds, Rahim Khan returned from the fields a little earlier than usual. He found a group of children playing on the road. They ran away as they saw him, and even left their shoes behind in their haste. In vain did Rahim Khan shout 'Why are you running away? I am not going to beat you.' Meanwhile, it had started drizzling and he hurried homewards to tie up the bullocks before the big downpour came.

Entering his hut, Rahim Khan lighted the earthen-ware oil lamp and placed some crumbs of bread for the sparrows before he prepared his own dinner. 'Oh, Nuru, Oh, Bundu,' he shouted, but the sparrows did not come out. Anxious to find out what had happened to his friends, he peeped into the nest and found the quartet scared and sitting huddled up within their feathers. At the very spot where the nest lay, the roof was leaking. Rahim Khan took a ladder and went out in the pouring rain to repair the damage. By the time the job was satisfactorily done he was thoroughly drenched. As he sat on the cot Rahim Khan sneezed but he did not heed the warning and went to sleep. Next morning he awoke with a high fever.

When the villagers did not see him going to the fields for several days they grew anxious and some of them came to see what was the matter. Through a crack in the door they saw him lying on the cot talking, so they thought, to himself, 'Oh Bundu, Oh Nuru, who will feed you when I am gone?'

The peasants shook their heads sympathetically. 'Poor fellow,' they said, 'He has gone mad. We will send for his wife to look after him.'

Next morning when Rahim Khan's wife, anxious and weeping, came with her sons, a group of neighbours collected in sympathy. The door was locked from the inside and in spite of loud knocking no one opened it. When they broke their way in they found the large and gaunt frame of Rahim Khan lying dead in the brooding silence of the room, broken only by the fluttering of four sparrows.

From *Indian Literature* (London), 1938

KHUSHWANT SINGH

Novelist, historian and editor, Khushwant Singh was born in Hadali (now in Pakistan) in 1915. He received his university education at St Stephen's College, Delhi, and Government College, Lahore, from where he went to London and obtained his LL.B. and Bar-at-law in 1938. From 1947 to 1951 he was Press Attaché at the Indian High Commissions in London and Ottawa. He published his first fictional work, *The Mark of Vishnu and Other Stories*, in 1950. But it was *Train to Pakistan* (1955) which brought him into prominence and started him on a writing career which includes not only fictional works such as *I Shall Not Hear the Nightingale* (1959) and *A Bride for the Sahib and Other Stories* (1967), but also some of the most authoritative studies of Sikh history and religion, notably *A History of the Sikhs, 1469–1964* (1963–6). After visiting academic appointments at Princeton, Swarthmore, and other universities from 1964 to 1969, he took over as editor of *The Illustrated Weekly of India*. Currently, he is editor of *The Hindustan Times*, and a nominated member of the Rajya Sabha.

'Karma' holds to ridicule the slavish mentality of those Indians who disowned their own people in the days of the Raj, and aped their British masters. Sir Mohan Lal, flaunting a Balliol College tie and a copy of *The Times*, makes himself comfortable in an empty first-class coupé of a train. His unsophisticated fat wife, whom he considers unworthy of being seen with him in the company of sahibs, is by herself in an inter-class compartment chewing betel. While Sir Mohan is hoping that some Englishman with whom he could talk about 'dear old England' will join him in the coupé, two tommies appear, call him a nigger and throw him out. The train pulls out of the station, and Sir Mohan gets a glimpse of his wife sitting complacently and spitting 'a jet of red dribble'.

Widely anthologized, 'The Mark of Vishnu' makes its point as stringently as 'Karma'. Khushwant Singh's purpose in the story is to expose the folly of superstition and blind reverence. The servant Gunga Ram, a devotee of Vishnu, feeds a King Cobra every night. One day the children of the house, who do not share his reverence, 'kill' the cobra. They put him in a tin and give it to their science teacher. When the teacher opens the tin, the snake, not quite dead, springs up and drags himself to the door. He finds his path blocked by Gunga Ram, who is prostrate before him. The enraged snake bites him on the forehead, leaving a V-mark, the mark of Vishnu, which Gunga Ram used to smear on his forehead every morning with sandalwood paste.

Karma

Sir Mohan Lal looked at himself in the mirror of a first-class waiting-room at the railway station. The mirror was obviously made in India. The red oxide at its back had come off at several places and long lines of translucent glass cut across its surface. Sir Mohan smiled at the mirror with an air of pity and patronage.

The mirror smiled back at Sir Mohan.

'You are a bit of all right, old chap,' it said. 'Distinguished, efficient—even handsome. That neatly trimmed moustache—the suit from Saville Row with the carnation in the button-hole—the aroma of eau de cologne, talcum powder, and scented soap all about you! Yes, old fellow, you are a bit of all right.'

Sir Mohan threw out his chest, smoothed his Balliol tie for the umpteenth time and waved a goodbye to the mirror.

He glanced at his watch. There was still time for a quick one. 'Koi hai?'

A bearer in white livery appeared through a wire-gauze door.

'Ek chota,' ordered Sir Mohan, and sank into a large cane chair to drink and ruminate.

Outside the waiting-room Sir Mohan Lal's luggage lay piled along the wall. On a small grey steel trunk Lachmi, Lady Mohan Lal, sat chewing a betel leaf and fanning herself with a newspaper. She was short and fat and in her middle forties. She wore a dirty white sari with a red border. On one side of her nose glistened a diamond nose-ring and she had several gold bangles on her arms. She had been talking to the bearer until Sir Mohan had summoned him inside. As soon as he had gone, she hailed a passing railway coolie.

'Where does the zenana stop?'

'Right at the end of the platform.'

The coolie flattened his turban to make a cushion, hoisted the steel trunk on his head, and moved down the platform. Lady Lal picked up her brass tiffin-carrier and ambled along behind him. On the way she stopped by a hawker's stall to replenish her silver betel-leaf case, and then joined the coolie. She sat down on her steel trunk (which the coolie had put down) and started talking to him.

'Are the trains very crowded on these lines?'

'These days all trains are crowded, but you'll find room in the zenana.'

'Then I might as well get over the bother of eating.'

Lady Lal opened the brass carrier and took out a bundle of cramped chapatis and some mango pickle. While she ate, the coolie sat opposite her on his haunches, drawing lines in the gravel with his finger.

'Are you travelling alone, sister?'

'No, I am with my master, brother. He is in the waiting-room. He travels first class. He is a vizier and a barrister, and meets many officers and Englishmen in the trains—and I am only a native woman. I can't understand English and don't know their ways, so I keep to my zenana inter-class.'

Lachmi chatted away merrily. She was fond of a little gossip and had no one to talk to at home. Her husband never had any time to spare for her. She lived in the upper storey of the house and he on the ground floor. He did not like her poor illiterate relatives hanging about his bungalow, so they never came. He came up to her once in a while at night and stayed for a few minutes. He just ordered her about in anglicized Hindustani, and she obeyed passively. These nocturnal visits had, however, borne no fruit.

The signal came down and the clanging of the bell announced the approaching train. Lady Lal hurriedly finished off her meal.

She got up, still licking the stone of the pickled mango. She emitted a long, loud belch as she went to the public tap to rinse her mouth and hands. After washing she dried her mouth and hands with the loose end of her sari and walked back to her steel trunk, belching and thanking the gods for the favour of a filling meal.

The train steamed in. Lachmi found herself facing an almost empty inter-class zenana compartment next to the guard's van, at the tail end of the train. The rest of the train was packed. She heaved her squat, bulky frame through the door and found a seat by the window. She produced a two-anna bit from a knot in her sari and dismissed the coolie. She then opened her betel case and made herself two betel leaves charged with a red and white paste, minced betelnuts and cardamoms. These she thrust into her mouth till her cheeks bulged on both sides. Then she rested her chin on her hands and sat gazing idly at the jostling crowd on the platform.

The arrival of the train did not disturb Sir Mohan Lal's *sang-froid*. He continued to sip his Scotch and ordered the bearer to tell him when he had moved the luggage to a first-class compartment. Excitement, bustle, and hurry were exhibitions of bad breeding, and Sir Mohan was eminently well-bred. He wanted everything 'tickety-boo' and orderly. In his five years abroad, Sir Mohan had acquired the manners and attitudes of the upper classes. He rarely spoke Hindustani. When he did, it was like an Englishman's—only the very necessary words and properly anglicized. But he fancied his English, finished and refined at no less a place than the University of Oxford. He was fond of conversation, and like a cultured Englishman he could talk on almost any subject—books, politics, people. How frequently had he heard English people say that he spoke like an Englishman!

Sir Mohan wondered if he would be travelling alone. It was a Cantonment and some English officers might be on the train. His heart warmed at the prospect of an impressive conversation. He never showed any sign of eagerness to talk to the English as most Indians did. Nor was he loud, aggressive, and opinionated like them. He went about his business with an expressionless matter-of-factness. He would retire to his corner by the window and get out a copy of *The Times*. He would fold it in a way in which the name of the paper was visible to others while he did the crossword puzzle. *The Times* always attracted attention. Someone would like to borrow it when he put it aside with a gesture signifying, 'I've finished with it.' Perhaps someone would recognize his Balliol tie which he always wore while travelling. That would open a vista leading to a fairyland of Oxford colleges, masters, dons, tutors, boat races, and rugger matches. If both *The Times* and the tie failed, Sir Mohan would 'Koi hai' his bearer to get the Scotch out. Whisky never failed with Englishmen. Then followed Sir Mohan's handsome gold cigarette case filled with English cigarettes. English cigarettes in India? How on earth did he get them? Sure, he didn't mind? And Sir Mohan's understanding smile—of course he didn't. But could he use the Englishman as a medium to commune with his dear old England? Those five years of grey bags and gowns, of sports blazers and mixed doubles, of dinners at the Inns of Court and nights with Piccadilly prostitutes. Five years of a crowded glorious life. Worth far more than the forty-five in India with his dirty, vulgar countrymen, with sordid details of the road to success, of nocturnal visits to the upper storey and all-too-brief sexual acts with obese old Lachmi, smelling of sweat and raw onions.

Sir Mohan's thoughts were disturbed by the bearer announcing the installation of the Sahib's luggage in a first-class coupé next to the engine. Sir Mohan walked to his coupé with a studied gait. He was dismayed. The compartment was empty. With a sigh he sat down in a corner and opened the copy of *The Times* he had read several times before.

Sir Mohan looked out of the window down the crowded platform. His face lit up as he saw two English soldiers trudging along, looking in all the compartments for room. They had their haversacks slung behind their backs and walked unsteadily. Sir Mohan decided to welcome them, even though they were entitled to travel only second class. He would speak to the guard.

One of the soldiers came up to the last compartment and stuck his face through the window. He surveyed the compartment and noticed the unoccupied berth.

' 'Ere, Bill,' he shouted, 'one 'ere.'

His companion came up, also looked in, and looked at Sir Mohan.

'Get the nigger out,' he muttered to his companion.

They opened the door, and turned to the half-smiling, half-protesting Sir Mohan.

'Reserved!' yelled Bill.

'Janata—Reserved. Army Fauj,' exclaimed Jim, pointing to his khaki shirt.

'Ek dum jao—get out!'

'I say, I say, surely,' protested Sir Mohan in his Oxford accent.

The soldiers paused. It almost sounded like English, but they knew better than to trust their inebriated ears. The engine whistled and the guard waved his green flag.

They picked up Sir Mohan's suitcase and flung it onto the platform. Then followed his thermos-flask, suitcase, bedding, and *The Times*. Sir Mohan was livid with rage.

'Preposterous, preposterous,' he shouted hoarse with anger. 'I'll have you arrested—guard, guard!'

Bill and Jim paused again. It did sound like English, but it was too much of the King's for them.

'Keep yer ruddy mouth shut!' And Jim struck Sir Mohan flat on the face.

The engine gave another short whistle and the train began to move. The soldiers caught Sir Mohan by the arms and flung him out of the train. He reeled backwards, tripped on his bedding, and landed on the suitcase.

'Toodle-oo!'

Sir Mohan's feet were glued to the earth and he lost his speech. He stared at the lighted windows of the train going past him in quickening tempo. The tail end of the train appeared with a red light and the guard standing in the open doorway with the flags in his hands.

In the inter-class zenana compartment was Lachmi, fair and fat, on whose nose the diamond nose-ring glistened against the station lights. Her mouth was bloated with betel saliva which she had been storing up to spit as soon as the train had cleared the station. As the train sped past the lighted part of the platform, Lady Lal spat and sent a jet of red dribble flying across like a dart.

From *The Mark of Vishnu and Other Stories*, 1950

The Mark of Vishnu

'This is for the Kala Nag,' said Gunga Ram, pouring the milk into the saucer. 'Every night I leave it outside the hole near the wall and it's gone by the morning.'

'Perhaps it is the cat,' we youngsters suggested.

'Cat!' said Gunga Ram with contempt. 'No cat goes near that hole. Kala Nag lives there. As long as I give him milk, he will not bite anyone in this house. You can all go about with bare feet and play where you like.'

We were not having any patronage from Gunga Ram.

'You're a stupid old Brahmin,' I said. 'Don't you know snakes don't drink milk? At least one couldn't drink a saucerful every day. The teacher told us that a snake eats only once in several days. We saw a grass snake which had just swallowed a frog. It stuck like a blob in its throat and took several days to dissolve and go down its tail. We've got dozens of them in the lab in methylated spirit. Why, last month the teacher bought one from a snake-charmer which could run both ways. It had another head with a pair of eyes at the tail. You should have seen the fun when it was put in the jar. There wasn't an empty one in the lab. So the teacher put it in one which had a Russell's viper. He caught its two ends with a pair of forceps, dropped it in the jar, and quickly put the lid on. There was an absolute storm as it went round and round in the glass tearing the decayed viper into shreds.'

Gunga Ram shut his eyes in pious horror.

'You will pay for it one day. Yes, you will.'

It was no use arguing with Gunga Ram. He, like all good Hindus, believed in the Trinity of Brahma, Vishnu, and Siva—the creator, preserver, and destroyer. Of these he was most devoted to Vishnu. Every morning he smeared his forehead with a V-mark in sandalwood paste to honour the deity. Although a Brahmin, he was illiterate and full of superstition. To him, all life was sacred, even if it was of a serpent or scorpion or centipede. Whenever he saw one he quickly shoved it away lest we kill it. He picked up wasps we battered with our badminton rackets and tended their damaged wings. Sometimes he got stung. It never seemed to shake his faith. The more dangerous the animal, the more devoted Gunga Ram was to its existence. Hence the regard for snakes; above all, the cobra, who was the Kala Nag.

'We will kill your Kala Nag if we see him.'

'I won't let you. It's laid a hundred eggs and if you kill it all the eggs will become cobras and the house will be full of them. Then what will you do?'

'We'll catch them alive and send them to Bombay. They milk them there for anti-snake-bite serum. They pay two rupees for a live cobra. That makes two hundred rupees straightaway.'

'Your doctors must have udders. I never saw a snake have any. But don't you dare touch this one. It is a phannyar—it is hooded. I've seen it. It's three hands long. As for its hood!' Gunga Ram opened the palms of his hands and his head swayed from side to side. 'You should see it basking on the lawn in the sunlight.'

'That just proves what a liar you are. The phannyar is the male, so it couldn't have laid the hundred eggs. You must have laid the eggs yourself.'

The party burst into peals of laughter.

'Must be Gunga Ram's eggs. We'll soon have a hundred Gunga Rams.'

Gunga Ram was squashed. It was the lot of a servant to be constantly squashed. But having the children of the household make fun of him was too much even for Gunga Ram. They were constantly belittling him with their new-fangled ideas. They never read their scriptures. Nor even what the Mahatma said about non-violence. It was just shotguns to kill birds and the jars of methylated spirit to drown snakes. Gunga Ram would stick to his faith in the sanctity of life. He would feed and protect snakes because snakes were the most vile of God's creatures on earth. If you could love them, instead of killing them, you proved your point.

What the point was which Gunga Ram wanted to prove was not clear. He just proved it by leaving the saucerful of milk by the snake hole every night and finding it gone in the morning.

One day we saw Kala Nag. The monsoons had burst with all their fury and it had rained in the night. The earth which had lain parched and dry under the withering heat of the summer sun was teeming with life. In little pools frogs croaked. The muddy ground was littered with crawling worms, centipedes, and velvety lady-birds. Grass had begun to show and the banana leaves glistened bright and glossy green. The rain had flooded Kala Nag's hole. He sat in an open patch on the lawn. His shiny black hood glistened in the sunlight. He was big—almost six feet in length, and rounded and fleshy, as my wrist.

'Looks like a King Cobra. Let's get him.'

Kala Nag did not have much of a chance. The ground was slippery and all the holes and gutters were full of water. Gunga Ram was not at home to help.

Armed with long bamboo sticks, we surrounded Kala Nag before he even scented the danger. When he saw us his eyes turned a fiery red and he hissed and spat on all sides. Then like lightning Kala Nag made for the banana grove.

The ground was too muddy and he slithered. He had hardly gone five yards when a stick caught him in the middle and broke his back. A volley of blows reduced him to a squishy-squashy pulp of black and white jelly, spattered with blood and mud. His head was still undamaged.

'Don't damage the hood,' yelled one of us. 'We'll take Kala Nag to school.'

So we slid a bamboo stick under the cobra's belly and lifted him on the end of the pole. We put him in a large biscuit tin and tied it up with string. We hid the tin under a bed.

At night I hung around Gunga Ram waiting for him to get his saucer of milk. 'Aren't you going to take any milk for the Kala Nag tonight?'

'Yes,' answered Gunga Ram irritably. 'You go to bed.'

He did not want any more argument on the subject.

'He won't need the milk any more.'

Gunga Ram paused.

'Why?'

'Oh, nothing. There are so many frogs about. They must taste better than your milk. You never put any sugar in it anyway.'

The next morning Gunga Ram brought back the saucer with the milk still in it. He looked sullen and suspicious.

'I told you snakes like frogs better than milk.'

Whilst we changed and had breakfast Gunga Ram hung around us. The school bus came and we clambered into it with the tin. As the bus started we held out the tin to Gunga Ram.

'Here's your Kala Nag. Safe in this box. We are going to put him in spirit.'

We left him standing speechless, staring at the departing bus.

There was great excitement in the school. We were a set of four brothers, known for our toughness. We had proved it again.

'A King Cobra.'

'Six feet long.'

The tin was presented to the science teacher.

It was on the teacher's table, and we waited for him to open it and admire our kill. The teacher pretended to be indifferent and set us some problems to work on. With studied matter-of-factness he fetched his forceps and a jar with a banded Krait lying curled in muddy methylated spirit. He began to hum and untie the cord around the box.

As soon as the cord was loosened the lid flew into the air, just missing the teacher's nose. There was Kala Nag. His eyes burnt like embers and his hood was taut and undamaged. With a loud hiss he went for the teacher's face. The teacher pushed himself back on the chair and toppled over. He fell on the floor and stared at the cobra, petrified with fear. The boys stood up on their desks and yelled hysterically.

Kala Nag surveyed the scene with his bloodshot eyes. His forked tongue darted in and out excitedly. He spat furiously and then made a bid for freedom. He fell out of the tin on to the floor with a loud plop. His back was broken in several places and he dragged himself painfully to the door. When he got to the threshold he drew himself up once again with his hood outspread to face another danger.

Outside the classroom stood Gunga Ram with a saucer and a jug of milk. As soon as he saw Kala Nag come up he went down on his knees. He poured the milk into the saucer and placed it near the threshold. With hands folded in prayer he bowed his head to the ground craving forgiveness. In desperate fury, the cobra hissed and spat and bit Gunga Ram all over the head—then with great effort dragged himself into a gutter and wriggled out of view.

Gunga Ram collapsed with his hands covering his face. He groaned in agony. The poison blinded him instantly. Within a few minutes he turned pale and blue and froth appeared in his mouth. On his forehead were little drops of blood. These the teacher wiped with his handkerchief. Underneath was the V-mark where the Kala Nag had dug his fangs.

From *The Mark of Vishnu and
Other Stories,* 1950

RUSKIN BOND

Ruskin Bond was born in Kasauli, Himachal Pradesh, in 1934 and had his schooling at Bishop Cotton School, Simla. When he was twenty, he took up writing as a full-time occupation. In 1956 he published his first novel, *The Room on the Roof*, for which he was awarded the Llewellyn Rhys Memorial Prize. His other fictional works are *The Neighbour's Wife and Other Stories* (1968), *My First Love and Other Stories* (1968), *Angry River* (1972), *The Blue Umbrella* (1974), *The Man-eater of Manjari and Other Stories* (1974). The film *Junoon*, directed by Shyam Benegal, is based on one of his stories. He has written many books for children, and was fiction editor of *Imprint* for several years. He has lived in Mussoorie for the last twelve years. 'Once you have lived with the mountains,' he says, 'you belong to them.'

'The Night Train at Deoli' is one of Ruskin Bond's earliest stories and also one of his favourites. It recaptures with the right mixture of sentiment and objectivity the narrator's boyhood love for a girl selling baskets at a wayside railway station. He has seen her only twice on the platform at Deoli (where the train stops for ten minutes) while on his sojourns to Dehra Dun to spend his summer vacations. On the second occasion he tells her he will come again, and asks her if she would be there. She nods assent. But she is gone, and he can never summon up enough courage to break his journey at Deoli and find out what happened to her. The brief encounter with the girl has taken on the proportions of a beautiful dream which, the narrator knows only too well, would be lost if he were to dig beneath the surface.

The Night Train at Deoli

When I was at college I used to spend my summer vacations in Dehra, at my grandmother's place. I would leave the plains early in May and return late in July. Deoli was a small station about thirty miles from Dehra: it marked the beginning of the heavy jungles of the Indian Terai.

The train would reach Deoli at about five in the morning, when the station would be dimly lit with electric bulbs and oil-lamps, and the jungle across the railway tracks would just be visible in the faint light of dawn. Deoli had only one platform, an office for the stationmaster and a waiting-room. The platform boasted a tea stall, a fruit vendor, and a few stray dogs; not much else, because the train stopped there for only ten minutes before rushing on into the forests.

Why it stopped at Deoli, I don't know. Nothing ever happened there. Nobody got off the train and nobody got in. There were never any coolies on the platform. But the train would halt there a full ten minutes, and then a bell would sound, the guard would blow his whistle, and presently Deoli would be left behind and forgotten.

I used to wonder what happened in Deoli, behind the station walls. I always felt sorry for that lonely little platform, and for the place that nobody wanted to visit. I decided that one day I would get off the train at Deoli, and spend the day there, just to please the town.

I was eighteen, visiting my grandmother, and the night train stopped at Deoli. A girl came down the platform, selling baskets.

It was a cold morning and the girl had a shawl thrown across her shoulder. Her feet were bare and her clothes were old, but she was a young girl, walking gracefully and with dignity.

When she came to my window, she stopped. She saw that I was looking at her intently, but at first she pretended not to notice. She had a pale skin, set off by shiny black hair, and dark, troubled eyes. And then those eyes, searching and eloquent, met mine.

She stood by my window for some time and neither of us said anything. But when she moved on, I found myself leaving my seat and going to the carriage door. She noticed me at the door, and stood waiting on the platform, looking the other way. I walked across to the tea stall. A kettle was boiling over on a small fire, but the owner of the stall was busy serving tea somewhere on the train. The girl followed me behind the stall.

'Do you want to buy a basket?' she asked. 'They are very strong, made of the finest cane. . . .'

'No,' I said, 'I don't want a basket.'

We stood looking at each other for what seemed a very long time and then she said, 'Are you sure you don't want a basket?'

'All right, give me one,' I said, and I took the one on top and gave her a rupee, hardly daring to touch her fingers.

As she was about to speak, the guard blew his whistle; she said something, but it was lost in the clanging of the bell and the hissing of the engine. I had to run back to my compartment. The carriage shuddered and jolted forward.

I watched her as the platform slipped away. She was alone on the platform and she did not move, but she was looking at me and smiling. I watched her until the signal-box came in the way, and then the jungle hid the station, but I could still see her standing there alone. . . .

I sat up awake for the rest of the journey. I could not rid my mind of the picture of the girl's face and her dark, smouldering eyes.

But when I reached Dehra the incident became blurred and distant; for there were other things to occupy my mind. It was only when I was making the return journey, two months later, that I remembered the girl.

I was looking out for her as the train drew into the station and I felt an unexpected thrill when I saw her walking up the platform. I sprang off the footboard and waved to her.

When she saw me, she smiled. She was pleased that I remembered her. I was pleased that she remembered me. We were both pleased, and it was almost like a meeting of old friends.

She did not go down the length of the train selling baskets, but came straight to the tea stall; her dark eyes were suddenly filled with light. We said nothing for some time but we couldn't have been more eloquent. I felt the impulse to put her on the train there and then, and take her away with me; I could not bear the thought of having to watch her recede into the distance of Deoli station. I took the baskets from her hand and put them down on the ground. She put out her hand for one of them, but I caught her hand and held it.

'I have to go to Delhi,' I said.

She nodded. 'I do not have to go anywhere.'

The guard blew his whistle for the train to leave and how I hated the guard for doing that.

'I will come again,' I said. 'Will you be here?'

She nodded again, and, as she nodded, the bell clanged and the train slid forward. I had to wrench my hand away from the girl and run for the moving train.

This time I did not forget her. She was with me for the remainder of the journey, and for long after. All that year she was a bright, living thing. And when the college term finished I packed in haste and left for Dehra earlier than usual. My grandmother would be pleased at my eagerness to see her.

I was nervous and anxious as the train drew into Deoli, because I was wondering what I should say to the girl, and what I should do; I was determined that I wouldn't stand helplessly before her, hardly able to speak or do anything about my feelings.

The train came to Deoli, and I looked up and down the platform, but I could not see the girl anywhere.

I opened the door and stepped off the footboard. I was deeply disappointed, and overcome by a sense of foreboding. I felt I had to do something, and so I ran up to the station-master and said, 'Do you know the girl who used to sell baskets here?'

'No, I don't,' said the station-master. 'And you'd better get on the train if you don't want to be left behind.'

But I paced up and down the platform, and stared over the railings at the station yard; all I saw was a mango tree and a dusty road leading into the jungle. Where did the road go? The train was moving out of the station, and I had to run up the platform and jump for the door of my compartment. Then, as the train gathered speed and rushed through the forests, I sat brooding in front of the window.

What could I do about finding a girl I had seen only twice, who had hardly spoken to me, and about whom I knew nothing

—absolutely nothing—but for whom I felt a tenderness and responsibility that I had never felt before?

My grandmother was not pleased with my visit after all, because I didn't stay at her place more than a couple of weeks. I felt restless and ill-at-ease. So I took the train back to the plains, meaning to ask further questions of the station-master at Deoli.

But at Deoli there was a new station-master. The previous man had been transferred to another post within the past week. The new man didn't know anything about the girl who sold baskets. I found the owner of the tea stall, a small, shrivelled-up man, wearing greasy clothes, and asked him if he knew anything about the girl with the baskets.

'Yes, there was such a girl here, I remember quite well,' he said. 'But she has stopped coming now.'

'Why?' I asked. 'What happened to her?'

'How should I know?' said the man. 'She was nothing to me.'

And once again I had to run for the train.

As Deoli platform receded, I decided that one day I would have to break journey there, spend a day in the town, make enquiries, and find the girl who had stolen my heart with nothing but a look from her dark, impatient eyes.

With this thought I consoled myself throughout my last term in college. I went to Dehra again in the summer and when, in the early hours of the morning, the night train drew into Deoli station, I looked up and down the platform for signs of the girl, knowing I wouldn't find her but hoping just the same.

Somehow, I couldn't bring myself to break journey at Deoli and spend a day there. (If it was all fiction or a film, I reflected, I would have got down and cleared up the mystery and reached a suitable ending for the whole thing.) I think I was afraid to do this. I was afraid of discovering what really happened to the girl. Perhaps she was no longer in Deoli, perhaps she was married, perhaps she had fallen ill. . . .

In the last few years I have passed through Deoli many times, and I always look out of the carriage window, half expecting to see the same unchanged face smiling up at me. I wonder what happens in Deoli, behind the station walls. But I will never break my journey there. I prefer to keep hoping and dreaming, and looking out of the window up and down that lonely platform, waiting for the girl with the baskets.

I never break my journey at Deoli, but I pass through as often as I can.

From *My First Love and Other Stories*, 1968

ANITA DESAI

Anita Desai was born in Mussoorie in 1937, and graduated from Miranda House, Delhi University, in 1957. Currently, she lives in New Delhi. Among her novels are *Cry, the Peacock* (1963), *Voices in the City* (1965), *Bye-bye, Blackbird* (1971), *Where Shall We Go This Summer?* (1975) and *Fire on the Mountain* (1977), which won her the Sahitya Akademi Award in 1978, and *Clear Light of Day* (1980). 'My novels', writes Anita Desai, 'are no reflection of Indian society, politics or character. They are part of my private effort to seize upon the raw material of life, and to mould it and impose on it a design. . . .'

'A Devoted Son' has quite a few of the qualities for which Anita Desai has earned a name: lucid prose, subtle character-ization and gentle irony. Rakesh, who lives completely by the rules, fulfils his parents' every dream. He excels in his studies and returns from the U.S.A. with an M.D. (minus an American wife, much to his mother's satisfaction) to set up his own clinic in his small home town. He nurses his mother in her last illness, and after she has gone he gives his ageing father the full benefits of filial duty and medical science. He puts his father on a strict diet after the latter's first illness, subjecting him to large quanti-ties of powders, pills and mixtures. This results in a sea change in the old man's attitude towards his once beloved son. He finds life a chore and wishes to die. But the devoted son will not have it so. 'I have my duty to you, Papa,' he says. In these few words lie the germs of the author's message. Duty without humanity or love is meaningless.

A Devoted Son

When the results appeared in the morning papers, Rakesh scanned them, barefoot and in his pyjamas at the garden gate, then went up the steps to the veranda where his father sat sipping his morning tea and bowed down to touch his feet.

'A first division, son?' his father asked, beaming, reaching for the papers.

'At the top of the list, Papa,' Rakesh murmured, as if awed. 'First in the country.'

Bedlam broke loose then. The family whooped and danced. The whole day long visitors streamed into the small yellow house at the end of the road, to congratulate the parents of this Wunderkind, to slap Rakesh on the back and fill the house and garden with the sounds and colours of a festival. There were garlands and halwa, party clothes and gifts (enough fountain pens to last years, even a watch or two), nerves and temper and joy, all in a multicoloured whirl of pride and great shining vistas newly opened: Rakesh was the first son in the family to receive an education, so much had been sacrificed in order to send him to school and then medical college, and at last the fruits of their sacrifice had arrived, golden and glorious.

To everyone who came to him to say, 'Mubarak, Varmaji, your son has brought you glory,' the father said, 'Yes, and do you know what is the first thing he did when he saw the results this morning? He came and touched my feet. He bowed down and touched my feet.' This moved many of the women in the crowd so much that they were seen to raise the ends of their saris and dab at their tears while the men reached out for the betel leaves and sweetmeats that were offered around on trays and shook their heads in wonder and approval of such exemplary filial behaviour. 'One does not often see such behaviour in sons any more,' they all agreed, a little enviously perhaps. Leaving the house, some of the women said, sniffing, 'At least on such an occasion they might have served pure ghee sweets,' and some of the men said, 'Don't you think old Varma was giving himself airs? He needn't think we don't remember that he came from the vegetable market himself, his father used to sell vegetables, and he has never seen the inside of a school.' But there was more envy than rancour in their voices and it was, of course, inevitable—not every son in that shabby little colony at the edge of the city was destined to shine as Rakesh shone, and who knew that better than the parents themselves?

And that was only the beginning, the first step in a great, sweeping ascent to the radiant heights of fame and fortune. The thesis he wrote for his M.D. brought Rakesh still greater glory, if only in select medical circles. He won a scholarship. He went to the U.S.A. (that was what his father learnt to call it and taught the whole family to say—not America, which was what the ignorant neighbours called it, but, with a grand familiarity, 'the U.S.A.') where he pursued his career in the most prestigious of all hospitals and won encomiums from his American colleagues which were relayed to his admiring and glowing family. What was more, he came back, he actually returned to that small yellow house in the once-new but increasingly shabby colony, right at the end of the road where the rubbish vans tipped out their stinking contents for pigs to nose in and ragpickers to build their shacks on, all steaming and smoking just outside the neat wire fences and well-tended gardens. To this Rakesh returned and the first thing he did on entering the house was to slip out of the embraces of his sisters and brothers and bow down and touch his father's feet.

As for his mother, she gloated chiefly over the strange fact that he had not married in America, had not brought home a foreign wife as all her neighbours had warned her he would, for wasn't that what all Indian boys went abroad for? Instead he agreed, almost without argument, to marry a girl she had picked out for him in her own village, the daughter of a childhood friend, a plump and uneducated girl, it was true, but so old-fashioned, so placid, so complaisant that she slipped into the household and settled in like a charm, seemingly too lazy and too good-natured to even try and make Rakesh leave home and set up independently, as any other girl might have done. What was more, she was pretty—really pretty, in a plump, pudding way that only gave way to fat—soft, spreading fat, like warm wax—after the birth of their first baby, a son, and then what did it matter?

For some years Rakesh worked in the city hospital, quickly rising to the top of the administrative organization, and was made a director before he left to set up his own clinic. He took his parents in his car—a new, sky-blue Ambassador with a rear window full of stickers and charms revolving on strings—to see the clinic when it was built, and the large sign-board over the door on which his name was printed in letters of red, with a row of degrees and qualifications to follow it like so many little black slaves of the regent. Thereafter his fame seemed to grow just a little dimmer—or maybe it was only that everyone in town had grown accustomed to it at last—but it was also the beginning of his fortune for he now became known not only as the best but also the richest doctor in town.

However, all this was not accomplished in the wink of an eye. Naturally not. It was the achievement of a lifetime and it took up Rakesh's whole life. At the time he set up his clinic his father had grown into an old man and retired from his post at the kerosene dealer's depot at which he had worked for forty years, and his mother died soon after, giving up the ghost with a sigh that sounded positively happy, for it was her own son who ministered to her in her last illness and who sat pressing her feet at the last moment—such a son as few women had borne.

For it had to be admitted—and the most unsuccessful and most rancorous of neighbours eventually did so—that Rakesh was not only a devoted son and a miraculously good-natured man who contrived somehow to obey his parents and humour his wife and show concern equally for his children and his patients, but there was actually a brain inside this beautifully polished and formed body of good manners and kind nature and, in between ministering to his family and playing host to many friends and coaxing them all into feeling happy and grateful and content, he had actually trained his hands as well and emerged an excellent doctor, a really fine surgeon. How one man—and a man born to illiterate parents, his father having worked for a kerosene dealer and his mother having spent her life in a kitchen—had achieved, combined and conducted such a medley of virtues, no one could fathom, but all acknowledged his talent and skill.

It was a strange fact, however, that talent and skill, if displayed for too long, cease to dazzle. It came to pass that the most admiring of all eyes eventually faded and no longer blinked at his glory. Having retired from work and having lost his wife, the old father very quickly went to pieces, as they say. He developed so many complaints and fell ill so frequently and with such mysterious diseases that even his son could no longer make out when it was something of significance and when it was merely a peevish whim. He sat huddled on his string bed most of the day and developed an exasperating habit of stretching out suddenly and lying absolutely still, allowing the whole family to fly around him in a flap, wailing and weeping, and then suddenly sitting up, stiff and gaunt, and spitting out a big gob of betel juice as if to mock their behaviour.

He did this once too often: there had been a big party in the house, a birthday party for the youngest son, and the celebrations had to be suddenly hushed, covered up and hustled out of the way when the daughter-in-law discovered, or thought she discovered, that the old man, stretched out from end to end of his string bed, had lost his pulse; the party broke up, dissolved, even turned into a band of mourners, when the old man sat up and the distraught daughter-in-law received a gob of red spittle right on the hem of her new organza sari. After that no one much cared if he sat up cross-legged on his bed, hawking and spitting, or lay down flat and turned grey as a corpse. Except, of course, for that pearl amongst pearls, his son Rakesh.

It was Rakesh who brought him his morning tea not in one of the china cups from which the rest of the family drank, but in the old man's favourite brass tumbler, and sat at the edge of his bed, comfortable and relaxed with the string of his pyjamas dangling out from under his fine lawn night-shirt, and discussed or, rather, read out the morning news to his father. It made no difference to him that his father made no response apart from spitting. It was Rakesh, too, who, on returning from the clinic in the evening, persuaded the old man to come out of his room, as bare and desolate as a cell, and take the evening air out in the garden, beautifully arranging the pillows and bolsters on the divan in the corner of the open veranda. On summer nights he saw to it that the servants carried out the old man's bed onto the lawn and himself helped his father down the steps and onto the bed, soothing him and settling him down for a nigh under the stars.

All this was very gratifying for the old man. What was not so gratifying was that he even undertook to supervise his father's diet. One day when the father was really sick, having ordered his daughter-in-law to make him a dish of sooji halwa and eaten it with a saucerful of cream, Rakesh marched into the room, not with his usual respectful step but with the confident and rather contemptuous stride of the famous doctor, and declared, 'No more halwa for you, Papa. We must be sensible, at your age. If you must have something sweet, Veena will cook you a little kheer, that's light, just a little rice and milk. But nothing fried, nothing rich. We can't have this happening again.'

The old man who had been lying stretched out on his bed, weak and feeble after a day's illness, gave a start at the very sound, the tone of these words. He opened his eyes—rather, they fell open with shock—and he stared at his son with disbelief that darkened quickly to reproach. A son who actually refused his father the food he craved? No, it was unheard of, it was incredible. But Rakesh had turned his back to him and was cleaning up the litter of bottles and packets on the medicine shelf and did not notice while Veena slipped silently out of the room with a little smirk that only the old man saw, and hated.

Halwa was only the first item to be crossed off the old man's diet. One delicacy after the other went—everything fried to begin with, then everything sweet, and eventually everything, everything that the old man enjoyed. The meals that arrived for him on the shining stainless steel tray twice a day were frugal to say the least—dry bread, boiled lentils, boiled vegetables and, if there was a bit of chicken or fish, that was boiled too. If he called for another helping—in a cracked voice that quavered theatrically—Rakesh himself would come to the door, gaze at him sadly and shake his head, saying, 'Now, Papa, we must be careful, we can't risk another illness, you know,' and although the daughter-in-law kept tactfully out of the way, the old man could just see her smirk sliding merrily through the air. He tried to bribe his grandchildren into buying him sweets (and how he missed his wife now, that generous, indulgent and illiterate cook), whispering, 'Here's fifty paise' as he stuffed the coins into a tight, hot fist. 'Run down to the shop at the crossroads and buy me thirty paise worth of jalebis, and you can spend the remaining twenty paise on yourself. Eh? Understand? Will you do that?' He got away with it once or twice but then was found out, the conspirator was scolded by his father and smacked by his mother and Rakesh came storming into the room, almost tearing his hair as he shouted through compressed lips, 'Now Papa, are you trying to turn my little son into a liar? Quite apart from spoiling your own stomach, you are spoiling him as well—you are encouraging him to lie to his own parents. You should have heard the lies he told his mother when she saw him bringing back those jalebis wrapped up in a filthy newspaper. I don't allow anyone in my house to buy sweets in the bazaar, Papa, surely you know that. There's cholera in the city, typhoid, gastroenteritis—I see these cases daily in the hospital, how can I allow my own family to run such risks?' The old man sighed and lay down in the corpse position. But that worried no one any longer.

There was only one pleasure left the old man now (his son's early morning visits and readings from the newspaper could no longer be called that) and those were visits from elderly neighbours. These were not frequent as his contemporaries were mostly as decrepit and helpless as he and few could walk the length of the road to visit him any more. Old Bhatia, next door, however, who was still spry enough to refuse, adamantly, to bathe in the tiled bathroom indoors and to insist on carrying out his brass mug and towel, in all seasons and usually at impossible hours, into the yard and bathe noisily under the garden tap, would look over the hedge to see if Varma were out on his veranda and would call to him and talk while he wrapped his dhoti about him and dried the sparse hair on his head, shivering with enjoyable exaggeration. Of course these conversations, bawled across the hedge by two rather deaf old men conscious of having their entire households overhearing them, were not very satisfactory but Bhatia occasionally came out of his yard, walked down the bit of road and came in at Varma's gate to collapse onto the stone plinth built under the temple tree. If Rakesh were at home he would help his father down the steps into the garden and arrange him on his night bed under the tree and leave the two old men to chew betel leaves and discuss the ills of their individual bodies with combined passion.

'At least you have a doctor in the house to look after you,' sighed Bhatia, having vividly described his martyrdom to piles.

'Look after me?' cried Varma, his voice cracking like an ancient clay jar. 'He—he does not even give me enough to eat.'

'What?' said Bhatia, the white hairs in his ears twitching. 'Doesn't give you enough to eat? Your own son?'

'My own son. If I ask him for one more piece of bread, he says no, Papa, I weighed out the ata myself and I can't allow you to have more than two hundred grammes of cereal a day. He weighs the food he gives me, Bhatia—he has scales to weigh it on. That is what it has come to.'

'Never,' murmured Bhatia in disbelief. 'Is it possible, even in this evil age, for a son to refuse his father food?'

'Let me tell you,' Varma whispered eagerly. 'Today the family was having fried fish—I could smell it. I called to my daughter-in-law to bring me a piece. She came to the door and said No . . .'

'Said No?' It was Bhatia's voice that cracked. A drongo shot out of the tree and sped away. 'No?'

'No, she said no, Rakesh has ordered her to give me nothing fried. No butter, he says, no oil—'

'No butter? No oil? How does he expect his father to live?'

Old Varma nodded with melancholy triumph. 'That is how he treats me—after I have brought him up, given him an education, made him a great doctor. Great doctor! This is the way great doctors treat their fathers, Bhatia,' for the son's sterling personality and character now underwent a curious sea change. Outwardly all might be the same but the interpretation had altered: his masterly efficiency was nothing but cold heart-lessness, his authority was only tyranny in disguise.

There was cold comfort in complaining to neighbours and, on such a miserable diet, Varma found himself slipping, weakening and soon becoming a genuinely sick man. Powders and pills and mixtures were not only brought in when dealing with a crisis like an upset stomach but became a regular part of his diet—became his diet, complained Varma, supplanting the natural foods he craved. There were pills to regulate his bowel movements, pills to bring down his blood pressure, pills to deal with his arthritis, and, eventually, pills to keep his heart beating. In between there were panicky rushes to the hospital, some humiliating experiences with the stomach pump and enema, which left him frightened and helpless. He cried easily, shrivelling up on his bed, but if he complained of a pain or even a vague, grey fear in the night, Rakesh would simply open another bottle of pills and force him to take one. 'I have my duty to you, Papa,' he said when his father begged to be let off.

'Let me be,' Varma begged, turning his face away from the pill on the outstretched hand, 'Let me die. It would be better. I do not want to live only to eat your medicines.'

'Papa, be reasonable.'

'I leave that to you,' the father cried with sudden spirit. 'Let me alone, let me die now, I cannot live like this.'

'Lying all day on his pillows, fed every few hours by his daughter-in-law's own hands, visited by every member of his family daily—and then he says he does not want to live "like this" ' Rakesh was heard to say, laughing, to someone outside the door.

'Deprived of food,' screamed the old man on the bed, 'his wishes ignored, taunted by his daughter-in-law, laughed at by his grandchildren—that is how I live.' But he was very old and weak and all anyone heard was an incoherent croak, some expressive grunts and cries of genuine pain. Only once, when old Bhatia had come to see him and they sat together under the temple tree, they heard his cry, 'God is calling me—and they won't let me go.'

The quantities of vitamins and tonics he was made to take were not altogether useless. They kept him alive and even gave him a kind of strength that made him hang on long after he

ceased to wish to hang on. It was as though he were straining
at a rope, trying to break it, and it would not break, it was still
strong. He only hurt himself, trying.

In the evening, that summer, the servants would come into
his cell, grip his bed, one at each end, and carry it out to the
veranda, there setting it down with a thump that jarred every
tooth in his head. In answer to his agonized complaints they
said the Doctor Sahib had told them he must take the evening
air and the evening air they would make him take—thump.
Then Veena, that smiling, hypocritical pudding in a rustling
sari, would appear and pile up the pillows under his head till he
was propped up stiffly into a sitting position that made his head
swim and his back ache. 'Let me lie down,' he begged, 'I can't
sit up any more.'

'Try, Papa, Rakesh said you can if you try,' she said, and
drifted away to the other end of the veranda where her transistor
radio vibrated to the lovesick tunes from the cinema that she
listened to all day.

So there he sat, like some stiff corpse, terrified, gazing out on
the lawn where his grandsons played cricket, in danger of
getting one of their hard-spun balls in his eye, and at the gate
that opened on to the dusty and rubbish-heaped lane but still
bore, proudly, a newly touched-up signboard that bore his son's
name and qualifications, his own name having vanished from
the gate long ago.

At last the sky-blue Ambassador arrived, the cricket game
broke up in haste, the car drove in smartly and the doctor, the
great doctor, all in white, stepped out. Someone ran up to take
his bag from him, others to escort him up the steps. 'Will you
have tea?' his wife called, turning down the transistor set, 'or
a Coca-Cola? Shall I fry you some samosas?' But he did not
reply or even glance in her direction. Ever a devoted son, he
went first to the corner where his father sat gazing, stricken, at
some undefined spot in the dusty yellow air that swam before
him. He did not turn his head to look at his son. But he stopped
gobbling air with his uncontrolled lips and set his jaw as hard
as a sick and very old man could set it.

'Papa,' his son said, tenderly, sitting down on the edge of the bed and reaching out to press his feet.

Old Varma tucked his feet under him, out of the way, and continued to gaze stubbornly into the yellow air of the summer evening.

'Papa, I'm home.'

Varma's hand jerked suddenly, in a sharp, derisive movement, but he did not speak.

'How are you feeling, Papa?'

Then Varma turned and looked at his son. His face was so out of control and all in pieces, that the multitude of expressions that crossed it could not make up a whole and convey to the famous man exactly what his father thought of him, his skill, his art.

'I'm dying,' he croaked. 'Let me die, I tell you.'

'Papa, you're joking,' his son smiled at him, lovingly. 'I've brought you a new tonic to make you feel better. You must take it, it will make you feel stronger again. Here it is. Promise me you will take it regularly, Papa.'

Varma's mouth worked as hard as though he still had a gob of betel in it (his supply of betel had been cut off years ago). Then he spat out some words, as sharp and bitter as poison, into his son's face. 'Keep your tonic—I want none—I want none—I won't take any more of—of your medicines. None. Never,' and he swept the bottle out of his son's hand with a wave of his own, suddenly grand, suddenly effective.

His son jumped, for the bottle was smashed and thick brown syrup had splashed up, staining his white trousers. His wife let out a cry and came running. All around the old man was hubbub once again, noise, attention.

He gave one push to the pillows at his back and dislodged them so he could sink down on his back, quite flat again. He closed his eyes and pointed his chin at the ceiling, like some dire prophet, groaning, 'God is calling me—now let me go.'

From *Games at Twilight and
Other Stories*, 1978

Glossary

ababeel: fork-tailed swallow, *Hirundo rustica rustica*; its nest is built of mud pellets, sometimes lined with straw and attached to the side of a beam or rafter in a house. The author has, however, translated the word as sparrows.

ablutions: ceremonial washing of person, hands or sacred vessels; water that has been used for this.

acha: yes.

alamgir: protector, emperor or master of the world.

Anglicized Hindustani: Hindustani (a blend of Hindi and Urdu) as spoken by Englishmen.

annas: coin denomination in India and Pakistan no longer in use. An anna was one-sixteenth of a rupee.

aoji: come (*ji* indicates respect).

ata: wheat flour.

Atharva-veda: See vedas.

babu: Hindu gentleman; clerk, half-Anglicized Hindu.

bachcha: young boy; here it means inexperienced.

bahin chod: rape-sister (term of abuse).

banya: trader; Hindu money-lender.

Bapu: Father; a term of respect occasionally used for elderly Hindu men.

betel leaf: leaves which Indians wrap around bits of areca nut and chew.

betelnuts: areca nut used in betel.

bhai: brother.

bhoos: the hissing sound a serpent makes when disturbed or about to attack.

bigha: measure of land, usually between half and three quarters of an acre.

bonda: fried savoury stuffed with vegetables.

Brahma: first deity of the Hindu trinity, the other two being Vishnu and Shiva.

brahmin: member of the Hindu priestly caste.

bren: light-weight quick-firing machine gun.

bungalow: thatched cottage of one floor. The term is now extended to any house that stands apart in its own grounds.

cantonment: area of town reserved for troops and government officials.

Cauvery: river in South India.

champak tree: small tree, sacred to Hindus and Buddhists, bearing fragrant, creamy-white flowers, *Michelia champaca*.

chapati: small round of unleavened bread, baked on a griddle.

charpai: light bedstead with mattress of string.

chaupal: shed or shaded spot, in which the village community meets for public business.

collyrium: black eye-lotion.

coupé: here, railway carriage for two persons.

Dassera: Hindu autumn festival, celebrated on the tenth day of Ashvin (usually in October) in honour of the goddess Durga and the god Rama.

dhal: (porridge or soup made from) split peas.

dhoti: loin-cloth worn by Hindus.

dosai: fried rice pancake.

D.S.P.: Deputy Superintendent of Police.

ek chota: one small peg. Used generally for whiskey.

ek dum jao: Hindi equivalent of 'Go away at once.'

fauj: army.

Five brothers: The five Pandava brothers who, with the help of Krishna, are victorious over the Kauravas in the great war between the descendants of Bharata. The war is described in the Sanskrit epic, the *Mahabharata*.

ghee: clarified butter.

gingelly oil: edible oil extracted from sesamum seeds.

guru: teacher, spiritual leader.

haat: temporary and periodic market; mart.

halwa: sweetmeat of milk, sugar, almonds and ghee.

Haré Ram: an invocation—'Oh God!'

havaldar: sergeant in the army; non-commissioned officer.

hé: Indian wives traditionally do not utter their husbands' names, referring to them, instead, by the personal pronoun 'hé'.

Hemavathy: river in Karnataka.

hookah: oriental tobacco-pipe; hubble-bubble.

Hosakéré: name of village; it means New Tank (or Lake).

huzoor: sir; term of respect.

Ishwar: God.

izzat: honour, reputation.

ja ja: go away.

jalebi: ring-shaped saffron-coloured sweetmeat.

jamadar: junior non-commissioned officer in the Indian army.

jawan: young man; private soldier in the Indian army.

jutka: two-wheeled vehicle drawn by horse.

kabadi: game between two teams of nine.

kafir: unbeliever; non-Muslim.

kala nag: black cobra, often an object of Hindu veneration.

kazi: Muslim judge or magistrate; one who performs a Muslim marriage ceremony.

kheer: sweetened milk and rice pudding.

kikar tree: the tree *Acacia arabica* yielding gum arabic.

koi hai: 'Is there anyone there?' Here, it means 'call'.

lallas: merchants.

lathi: long stick, often used by the police as a weapon.

linga: male sexual organ; venerated image of Shiva's.

madar chod: rape-mother (term of abuse)

Mahatma: M. K. Gandhi, revered nationalist leader of India (*maha*: great, *atma*: soul).

mai-bap: mother-father; paternal.

mohur: gold coin.

mufti: plain clothes as opposed to uniform.

mubarak: congratulations.

munshi: scribe, teacher, secretary.

nazar: ceremonial present.

neem tree: the tree *Azadirachta indica*, the leaves and bitter bark of which are used medicinally.

nikah: marriage; marriage ceremony.

nose-ring: ornament (resembling an ear-ring) worn by Indian women on one of the nostrils.

ohé: term of exclamation, often indicating grief, surprise, astonishment or lamentation.

paise: coin denomination of a rupee.

paltans: armed forces.

pan-biri: betel and biri (Indian equivalent of a cigarette) shop.

pani: water.

pariah: Hindu outcastes or untouchables.

patel: village headman.

phannyar: hooded king cobra.

pipal tree: the *Ficus religiosa* or holy fig tree.

puja-room: prayer room.

pundit: learned man, teacher (from the Sanskrit *pandita*, learned).

pyol: raised platform for sitting on, in South India.

rais: title, a prince or chief, often used in relation to subject.

rangroot: mispronunciation of 'recruit'.

red man: Englishman.

roti: bread.

saab (sahib): rough Hindi equivalent of 'mister' (pronounced as in 'car').

samosa: triangular fried pastry stuffed with meat or vegetables.

sardar: chieftain, boss. A term of respect often prefixed to the name of a Sikh.

sarkar: state, government. The term is loosely used to denote a man in authority.

sari: Hindu woman's principal garment, a long piece of silk or cotton cloth wrapped around the waist with one end draped over the shoulder.

seer: measure of weight, usually the fortieth part of a maund (a maund is another measure of weight, varying from 25 lbs in Madras to 80 lbs in Bengal).

sepoy: policeman.

serai: resthouse for travellers.

seth: term of respect indicating position or wealth.

Shiva: the third deity of the Hindu trinity.

sooji halwa: halwa made of coarsely ground flour.

Subbéhalli: name of village.

subedar: officer in the Indian army. In ranking order, the subedar is senior to the jamadar, and the latter is senior to the havildar.

takla: small spindle.

Talakamma: goddess of the village.

tehsildar: collector of revenue in *tehsil*, a subdivision of a district.

terai: foothills.

tiffin-carrier: several metal containers superimposed to carry courses of meal.

Udbhavamruti: god rising from the earth.

vedas: Hindu sacred books, the Rig, Sama, Yajur and Atharva veda.

Vishnu: second deity of the Hindu trinity.

wallah: dealer of a particular trade.

Yama Loka: world of Yama, Hindu god who judges the dead.

zenana: part of house reserved for women; here railway carriage reserved for women passengers.

zaildar: minor revenue officer who collects land-taxes from a few villages.